D0391051

The Perfect Plan

Elizabeth stared in disbelief as Brooke left the lunch line and walked toward their table. Brooke put her tray in front of the empty seat by Lila.

"Wait a minute, you can't sit there," said Amy.

"And why, may I ask, can't I sit here?" Brooke said.

"Look, there are plenty of other tables," suggested Lila. "Go ruin someone else's day. This seat's taken."

"That's funny." Brooke glared at the fifth chair. "It looks pretty empty to me."

"Well, it's not," said Elizabeth, trying to hold her temper. "We're saving it."

"That's right," Lila agreed suddenly. "It's reserved."

"Yes!" Suddenly Jessica came alive. She had come up with the perfect scheme. "That seat's saved for my sister."

"Your what?" Brooke looked confused. "What do you mean? Your sister's right here."

"My other sister," Jessica said. "Didn't you know? We're triplets. That seat's saved for Jennifer."

Elizebeth didn't like to lie. But for once, she felt that someone actually deserved to be on the wrong end of one of Jessica's crazy schemes. . . .

Bantam-Skylark Books in the SWEET VALLEY TWINS Series
Ask your bookseller for the books you have missed

SWEET VALLEY TWINS

The New Girl

Written by
Jamie Suzanne

Created by
FRANCINE PASCAL

A BANTAM SKYLARK BOOK®
TORONTO · NEW YORK · LONDON · SYDNEY · AUCKLAND

RL 4, 008–012

THE NEW GIRL
A Bantam Skylark Book / February 1987

Sweet Valley High and Sweet Valley Twins are trademarks of Francine Pascal

Conceived by Francine Pascal

Produced by Cloverdale Press Inc.

Cover art by James Mathewuse

Skylark Books is a registered trademark of Bantam Books, Inc.
Registered in U.S. Patent and Trademark Office and elsewhere.

All rights reserved.
Copyright © 1987 by Francine Pascal.
Cover art copyright © 1987 by Bantam Books, Inc.
This book may not be reproduced in whole or in part, by
mimeograph or any other means, without permission.
For information address: Bantam Books, Inc.

ISBN 0-553-15475-3

Published simultaneously in the United States and Canada

Bantam Books are published by Bantam Books, Inc. Its trade-
mark, consisting of the words "Bantam Books" and the por-
trayal of a rooster, is Registered in U.S. Patent and Trademark
Office and in other countries. Marca Registrada. Bantam
Books, Inc., 666 Fifth Avenue, New York, New York 10103.

PRINTED IN THE UNITED STATES OF AMERICA

O   09

For Alexandra Nardi

One

◇

"I've never had so much homework in my life!" Jessica Wakefield declared. "I'll never be able to finish it all and learn the new cheer in time for tomorrow's game."

"Well, Jess," her sister Elizabeth told her, "if you have to make a choice, my guess is you'll know that cheer inside out before bedtime."

The two girls were identical twins, with long blond hair and blue-green eyes. But Elizabeth knew that when it came to schoolwork, they might as well have been from different planets! Elizabeth loved to read and write, and almost never put off homework. Jessica, on the other hand, welcomed any excuse to get out of an assignment. Now, as they walked home together from Sweet Valley Middle School, Elizabeth was not surprised when her sister made an urgent request.

"Liz." Jessica turned toward her twin with a solemn expression on her pretty face. "There's only one person in the whole world who can help me out. You're the smartest person in sixth grade English. I'll bet it would take you no time at all to whip up a tiny little paragraph or two on the book I had to read."

"Jessica, do you mean you want me to do a book report for you?"

Jessica tossed her blond ponytail and shook her head vigorously. "Of course not, silly. I only meant you could sort of get it started while I practice. After all, you wouldn't want your little sister to be the worst cheerleader in the whole Booster Club, would you?"

Elizabeth had been born four minutes before Jessica, and the two girls always joked about her being the older one. Sometimes, though, she really did feel more mature and responsible than her headstrong twin. Elizabeth was so patient and far-sighted, while fun-loving Jessica seldom saw past the next good time! So Jessica always ran to Elizabeth when her talent for trouble landed her in hot water. Still, Elizabeth thought fondly, it was impossible to imagine life without her twin.

"Tell you what, Jess." Elizabeth knew now was the time to enlist her twin's cooperation on the next issue of their class newspaper. "I'll start on an outline for your report if you'll get me the interview I need for *The Sweet Valley Sixers*."

Jessica, who loved to read the latest gossip in the *Sixers*, had no interest at all in anything so time-consuming as working for the paper. "Who are you interviewing?" she asked cautiously.

"It'll be easy," Elizabeth assured her. "Mr. Bowman wants a special article to introduce the new sixth grade student. I told him you'd met her in the neighborhood. You know, the girl who moved into the Logginses' old house."

"You mean Disgusting Dennis?" Jessica stopped in the middle of the street and turned to face her sister. "You want me to talk to that obnoxious snob?" She hugged her books to her chest and looked solemnly into the face that was the mirror image of her own. "Liz, I will never speak to that girl again, except to tell her exactly what I think of her!"

"I know you and Brooke Dennis didn't exactly hit it off, Jess. But I just thought—"

"You must be crazy if you think I'm going to have anything to do with someone the whole school's going to be sorry they met." Jessica frowned, then announced firmly, "I'd rather do my own book report."

Brooke Dennis had gotten off on the worst foot with Jessica. Usually, Jessica was willing to go to any lengths to avoid doing her own homework, but not this time. Elizabeth still remembered the way Jessica described Brooke after accidentally meeting her on a walk through the neighborhood. "That girl," Jessica had announced, "is the nastiest person I've ever met!" Obviously she hadn't changed her mind.

"I went out of my way to introduce myself and be friendly," Jessica declared. "And she made it very clear she didn't want any friends. Why, she even insulted poor Sally in front of me." Sally was the dog Jessica had baby-sat for.

"Caroline Pearce says Brooke's father is a famous screenwriter, and he's spending a ton of money to redecorate their new house. She even heard that Brooke went to finishing school before her family moved to Sweet Valley."

Jessica's eyes flashed. "Disgusting Dennis is finished all right. I'm going to make sure that none of my friends have anything to do with her. And once *that* happens she might as well march right back to finishing school, because she'll be all washed up here!"

Elizabeth knew that her sister tended to form quick opinions of people, and sometimes they were unfair. Elizabeth, on the other hand, liked to give everyone a chance. "Maybe she's not really so bad, Jess. Caroline says—"

"How is Caroline Pearce such an expert on someone she's never even met?" Jessica interrupted. "Big mouth Pearce is nothing but a full-time gossip!"

"I know Caroline sometimes talks before she thinks, Jess," Elizabeth began. "But I'd sure rather listen to someone who has nice things to say than waste my energy hating someone I don't really know!"

As the twins headed up their driveway, Jessica decided the last thing she wanted was a fight with her sister. "Lizzie," she said in her best making-up voice, "let's not spoil a nice afternoon by talking about you-know-who." She broke into a sunny smile and trotted ahead of her sister as they neared the kitchen door. "Race you to the refrigerator!"

They piled into the bright Spanish-tiled

kitchen of the Wakefields' split-level ranch house. Elizabeth reached the refrigerator just as Jessica was diving into a box of assorted donuts and pastries. "Where on earth did *these* come from?" she asked, choosing a shiny donut from the carton. "I thought we ate everything in the house doing math homework last night." The day before the twins had spent several hours working their way through two bags of potato chips, six cans of root beer, and three chapters of their math books.

Just then their older brother, Steven, burst through the door behind them. "Hold it right there," he warned, pointing his fingers like guns. "One more bite and you'll both be eating dust. This is a stickup, and I'm the fastest shot in the West!"

"And the fastest chewer," Elizabeth added, stuffing a donut into her brother's mouth. Tall and dark, Steven looked a lot like Mr. Wakefield. And even though Steven was usually a giant pain, sometimes Elizabeth thought he could be funny.

Jessica seemed to be enjoying her brother's cowboy imitation, too. "Just because you're a big deal high school freshman," she teased, "doesn't mean you can tell us what to do." She poked a gun finger of her own into Steven's ribs and started to tickle him. "I'm keeping this loot, and I'd like to see the cowpoke who can stop me."

"Hey, you two. I'm serious. Mom told me she bought some desserts for a very important client, and I have a feeling that if these goodies are gone when she gets home from work, this is our last roundup."

Jessica and Elizabeth stared first at each other

and then at the half-empty box. Quickly, Jessica retied the string around the white bakery carton and jammed it back onto the refrigerator shelf. "Maybe Mom's client is on a diet," she said hopefully.

"I don't think so," announced an amused voice from the doorway. "In fact, he looks like a pretty hefty eater to me." They all turned to see their slim, blond mother slipping her briefcase onto a kitchen chair.

"Don't worry, though," said Mrs. Wakefield. "I've learned from experience that it pays to keep a spare on hand." Joining the three at the refrigerator, she opened the door and removed another big bakery carton from the very back. Carefully she placed the box on the counter and revealed the biggest lemon meringue pie any of them had ever seen.

"Wow!" Steven's gaze lingered on the huge dessert. "Your new client must be some big shot to rate such special treatment."

"Well, Mr. Dennis *is* an important screenwriter. He's asked my firm to decorate his home and his office. But he's also new in town, so I wanted to let him know how happy we are he's moved to Sweet Valley."

Once again the twins exchanged glances. But this time they weren't worrying about food. "Do you mean the same Dennises that are moving in down the street?" Elizabeth knew that her mother's work as an interior designer often meant interesting visitors. But this time, she was sure it meant nothing but trouble!

"You mean they're coming *here*? *Tonight*?" Jessica's aqua eyes were flashing angrily.

"In answer to both your questions, yes." Mrs. Wakefield carefully lifted the pie from its box and lowered it onto a glass serving plate. "And I'm willing to bet," she added, smiling at Steven, "that once you find out which movie script Mr. Dennis wrote, you'll be running for your autograph book."

"It couldn't be too great," Steven said casually. "Nobody important ever comes to live in Sweet Valley."

"I'm not so sure. I'd be willing to drive a little bit to make sure I always came home to Sweet Valley's blue sky and white beach. Anyway, that's how the writer of *Car Capers* feels."

"*Car Capers?*" Steven looked as though he'd just won a million dollars. "You mean the creator of the greatest movie of all time is going to be our neighbor? And he's actually going to come over here tonight?"

Jessica was not as impressed. She'd seen *Car Capers*, too. But she'd also seen their new neighbor's daughter, and nothing and nobody was going to make her like Brooke Dennis. "Well, it just goes to show that money and fame aren't everything," Jessica said flatly. "They couldn't even buy Mr. Important a human being for a daughter."

"Jessica, I have a feeling you might change your mind about Brooke Dennis over a piece of this pie tonight."

"I have a feeling I'd rather die." Jessica saw the shocked expressions around her and hurried to explain. "Brooke Dennis actually tried to kick Mrs. Bramble's dog when I was walking her one day." She grimaced, recalling the tall, well-dressed girl she'd tried to say hello to as she and Sally, Mrs. Bramble's aging cocker spaniel, strolled down the street. Jessica hadn't been prepared for the rude reception she got from Brooke Dennis.

"Why would anyone want to kick a harmless old dog like Sally?" Steven asked. He still had a soft spot in his heart for the old dog. The whole Wakefield family had adopted her for a weekend while her elderly owner visited her family. "Sally is half blind and she wouldn't hurt a flea."

"Apparently Sally wasn't enough of a thoroughbred to satisfy Brooke Dennis. The minute Sally started trying to lick her, Brooke went nuts." Jessica winced, remembering the way the girl had shoved the old dog away from her with the toe of her designer shoe. "Miss Snob said she was an expert on dogs and that Sally was a pretty poor specimen!"

Steven scooped up his basketball jersey and headed toward the door. "Well, even if she's twice as gross as you say, I can't wait to meet her dad. Besides, Jess, she might not be so bad once you get to know her. See you guys after practice."

As the screen door slammed behind her brother, Jessica couldn't help wondering why everyone was defending Brooke, even before meeting her. "Just you wait," she told her mother and Elizabeth.

And that was exactly what Elizabeth decided to do. Even though Elizabeth had met Brooke

Dennis briefly, and agreed that the girl was unpleasant, Elizabeth intended to give her a chance.

Later that afternoon, Elizabeth sat at her desk, writing an English paper while Jessica practiced cheering in front of the full-length mirror in her room. Ignoring her twin's concentration, Jessica stood behind the open door, barking out the Boosters' latest cheer. "Give me a C!"

Elizabeth covered her ears and tried to think about *Black Beauty*.

"Give me a T!"

She was sure Anna Sewell didn't have half the trouble writing her book that Elizabeth was having writing *about* it! She got up and walked to the bathroom that separated her room from Jessica's, slamming the door with as much emphasis as she could.

"Give me an O-R-Y! What have you got?"

I've got one paragraph, Elizabeth thought, *and that's all I'm going to get as long as this cheer lasts.*

"Sweet Victory!" Jessica roared from her room, cartwheeling suddenly through the door to her sister's room and finishing with a flying leap that landed her squarely in the middle of Elizabeth's bed. "It's just no good," she announced angrily, turning over on her stomach and dangling her long suntanned legs over the side. "I can't think of anything but how revolting tonight's going to be."

"I can't think of anything, period. Jess, will you please shut your door and try to keep it down? If I don't get this paper done, I won't even get the chance to make up my mind about this new girl. I'll have to stay in my room all night and forget about dessert."

"That's it, Liz! You just gave me the best excuse in the world for not seeing Brooke. I'll just say I have too much homework."

Elizabeth got up from her desk and sat on the bed beside her twin. "There's only one problem with that, little sister," she said with a laugh. "How do you expect anyone to believe that Jessica Wakefield lets homework stand in the way of lemon meringue pie?"

Jessica pouted. "I guess you're right. I'll just have to get sick then. Which shouldn't be too hard," she added, winking at Elizabeth. "I'm already feeling pretty rotten just thinking about Brooke Dennis. Do you know, Liz, she was actually wearing a skirt and stockings on a weekend? She looked like the cover of *Seventeen*."

"Well, that just makes her someone a lot of your friends should really like, doesn't it?" Elizabeth teased.

"Laugh all you want, Liz," Jessica warned her twin. "But you'll be sorry you didn't listen to me."

Mr. Wakefield poked his head through the doorway and smiled at the twins. "You'll both be sorry if you miss the great dinner your mother's got ready."

By the time the three got downstairs, Steven and Mrs. Wakefield had set the table. The smell of roast beef filled the kitchen. "Mm-mm," Elizabeth said appreciatively. "We got here just in time."

"Yeah," Steven said sarcastically, "just in time to get out of helping."

The meal was delicious, and Jessica was so intent on eating that she had forgotten all about their after-dinner guests until the door bell rang out. Elizabeth looked at her twin. Jessica's face registered surprise, then suddenly she doubled over in her seat.

"Ohh-h-h-h," she wailed, looking miserable. "I think I ate too much!" Her mother was already walking toward the door when Jessica brushed past her in a mad dash for the stairs. "Save a piece of pie for me," she yelled down from the top step. "Maybe I'll feel better later." She raced into her room and shut the door tight just as Henry Dennis and his daughter walked into the front hall.

Two

◇

"Welcome." Mrs. Wakefield smiled at the stout man and his tall, slender daughter. "We've been so looking forward to meeting Brooke."

The girl who followed Mrs. Wakefield and Mr. Dennis into the living room was very pretty. Brooke walked stiffly and with her nose in the air, but she still seemed very delicate, with huge brown eyes and soft brown curls.

When everyone had been introduced and was seated comfortably, Mr. Wakefield apologized. "I'm afraid you won't be meeting the whole family tonight. It seems dinner was too much for some of us."

"Well, I can understand that," Mr. Dennis told him. "Brooke and I just finished one of the biggest lobsters I've ever seen. And, quite frankly, I didn't have much help at all."

Brooke's pretty face fell and her big eyes narrowed. "I just didn't like it, that's all."

"That's all right." Mrs. Wakefield smiled. "It just means you'll have more room for this." She reached forward to cut the lemon meringue pie that was sitting on the coffee table.

"Wow! I've been thinking about this all night!" Steven waited impatiently while his mother served the guests first.

"No thank you." Brooke shook her head when Mrs. Wakefield offered her some pie.

"But it looks delicious, honey," Mr. Dennis said. "You hardly ate any dinner. Why don't you try some?"

"I liked the food back home," she replied, still frowning.

Brooke wasn't trying to win any popularity contests, Elizabeth thought. Still, she was probably just lonely and missed her old school friends. Elizabeth smiled at her. "Maybe you'd rather come upstairs to my room and listen to some records, Brooke. We've got the latest Johnny Buck album."

But Brooke folded her hands over her pleated paisley skirt. "I don't like Johnny Buck at all," she told Elizabeth coldly. "I only listen to classical music."

"I'm afraid I'm responsible for that," Henry Dennis explained. "You see, the only records we have at home are mine, and Brooke spends most of her time listening to them. I've tried to tell her she should get out more, spend time with people her own age . . ."

"If I spent time with people my own age, I'd be bored to tears!" Brooke looked pointedly at Eliz-

abeth and then glared at Steven when she heard
him chuckling.

As the evening wore on, Elizabeth lost all
sympathy for their snobbish visitor. The Wakefields tried again and again to make Brooke feel at
home, but nothing worked. When Mrs. Wakefield
asked Brooke what colors she wanted in her new
bedroom, she turned positively nasty.

"I don't need anyone's help to decorate my
room," she snapped angrily. "Besides, it will never
be as nice as my old one."

"It's always hard to move." Mr. Wakefield
smiled with understanding at Mr. Dennis. "But I'll
bet making a few new friends will change all that."

"I don't need a new room," she declared.
"And I don't need new friends either!"

Jessica was nearly crazy with curiosity by the
time the Dennises had left.

As soon as she heard Elizabeth come up the
stairs, she darted through their bathroom and
banged on her door.

"Tell me everything," she begged, dropping
onto the bed and perking up her ears.

"I can tell you one thing, Jess." Elizabeth
faced her sister. "If I don't get some work done on
my English paper, you're going to be in worse
trouble with me than you already are with Mom."

"Why, Liz," Jessica was all wide-eyed inno-
cence. "What on earth do you mean?"

"I mean that Mom knows very well that that
stomachache of yours was the worst act to hit town
since . . . Brooke Dennis!"

Jessica beamed. "I knew it! Wasn't she hideous? Wasn't she the absolute worst?"

"I have to admit you were right," Elizabeth confessed. "Brooke Dennis is the rudest person I've ever met." She shook her head, recalling the way Brooke had treated the whole family. "She didn't try to kick any dogs tonight, but she sure did her best to hurt everyone's feelings."

Jessica rolled her eyes dramatically and looked at the ceiling. "And just think, we're going to have to put up with her at school."

"Worse than that. We're going to have to walk to school *with* her."

"What?" Jessica was horrified. Suddenly gossiping about Brooke wasn't fun anymore.

"It's true. Brooke's starting school tomorrow. Her father asked Mom if we could show her the way and, of course, Mom said we'd be glad to."

"That's easy for Mom to say," moaned Jessica, her head buried now in Elizabeth's bedspread. "*She* doesn't have to be seen in the company of the biggest creep in the world! How am I ever going to explain this to the Unicorns?"

The Unicorns were an exclusive club to which Jessica belonged. Elizabeth knew how important the club was to her sister. Still, a group of girls who called themselves the Unicorns because they thought they were beautiful and special seemed pretty silly. "I guess the snob squad will really be disappointed in you, huh, Jess?"

"Come on, Lizzie. Just because my friends happen to be popular and are always in on the latest fashions, doesn't mean they're snobs."

"Maybe not," said Elizabeth. "But it sure does mean they spend too much time on gossip and boys and too little time being friendly." She turned to the work at her desk. "Besides, I'm much more interested in horses than Unicorns right now." Once again, she began to write as she leafed through the pages of the story about the beautiful black stallion. "After Brooke, even homework seems like fun!"

"Well," Jessica suggested breezily, "as long as you're having such a ball, maybe you could write two papers and have twice as much fun?"

"Nice try, little sister. But no chance. I need to go to bed early. Or else I'll never be patient enough to walk Brooke to school without blowing up at her on the way!"

Jessica got off the bed and headed reluctantly toward her own room. "Okay." She sighed. "If Mr. Bowman knew what I've been through, I'll bet he wouldn't even expect me to turn in a report." She sighed again, reminding Elizabeth of a soap-opera heroine. "I've already worked all week drawing a Nancy Drew poster for that silly old book fair. And, to top it off, I have to walk to school with the biggest creep in the world! Tomorrow, I'll be a social outcast. Unless . . ." She stopped suddenly, her face brightening. "Unless I still have my stomachache tomorrow and can't go to school."

Jessica began playing her scene in earnest. "It really would be for the best, Liz. I mean everyone's used to *you* being friendly with social rejects, but I can't afford to be seen with the wrong people." She paused dramatically at the door to her room. "Think what it would do to my reputation!"

Jessica cared a lot more than her sister did about being popular. Although the girls looked alike, they couldn't have been more different in their choice of friends. Jessica wanted to know only the prettiest, most popular girls, while Elizabeth chose friends who were interesting and independent. In the case of Brooke Dennis, though, the twins were in complete agreement.

"I know it won't be easy." Elizabeth was genuinely sympathetic. "*Disgusting Dennis* may not be good for your image, Jess, and she may not be good for my temper, but I'm afraid we can't get out of tomorrow. We'll just have to try and make the best of things."

But the best of things seemed remote when the twins woke up the next morning. Elizabeth turned over in bed and immediately remembered whom she was walking to school with. Determined to be patient, she got up and headed for the bathroom. She poked her head into Jessica's room and noticed that, as usual, her twin had turned off her clock radio and had snuggled back under her sheets.

"Rise and shine," she called cheerily as she brushed her teeth in front of the mirror.

"I can't," Jessica groaned from deeper under her covers. "I didn't sleep well at all. I had Brooke-mares all night."

Elizabeth laughed. "Well, if it will make you feel any better you can wear my new hair ribbon."

"You mean the white one?"

"Yes. I thought it might boost your spirits on the long walk with Brooke."

"Thanks, Liz. It'll go really well with my new purple sweater-vest. But don't count on me walking with that monster. I've got a plan." She raced into Elizabeth's room and took the white ribbon out of the top dresser drawer. Then, still in her nightgown, she posed in front of the bathroom mirror with her hair pulled up.

"Jess, Mom already promised Brooke's father we'd walk with her today." She watched her sister whirling and smiling into the glass. "You wouldn't want to ruin Mom's chances with a big client, would you?"

Jessica continued to look into the mirror. Suddenly, she frowned at her blond reflection. "Just look at those giant circles under my eyes. I look awful, and it's all from worrying about Brooke Dennis. I'll be the laughingstock of the school and I won't be able to face anybody ever again, especially the Unicorns!"

Elizabeth joined her sister at the mirror. "May I remind you, Jessica Wakefield," she scolded, "that we are identical twins? If you look hideous, then so do I."

Jessica hugged her sister. "If I look as good as you, Lizzie, then there's nothing to worry about!" She took off the ribbon and put it on Elizabeth's head. "Hey, why don't you go to school as me today? We can tell Mom that you're sick. She knows *you* would never lie about something like that."

Elizabeth burst into giggles. "So that's your scheme! I thought we agreed to stop switching places. Besides," she reminded Jessica, "you know very well that Mom can tell us apart. So hurry up and get dressed. We're *both* going to school today."

But Jessica was not someone who gave up easily. At breakfast Elizabeth realized her twin had already hatched another plan to avoid walking to school with Brooke. As soon as she'd devoured two poached eggs and polished off one of her special bacon sandwiches, Jessica leaped from the table and hurried upstairs to her room. A minute later she was back in the kitchen with a huge oaktag board. "How do you like my poster for the book fair?" she asked, holding the big sheet in front of her face.

Everyone agreed that the poster was coming along beautifully. Using magic markers and glitter glue, Jessica had traced the covers of her favorite books in the Nancy Drew mystery series.

"You've had a lot of patience with this display, honey." Mrs. Wakefield looked at the careful work with approval. "Even if it doesn't win a prize, you should be very proud."

"Oh, it will win all right," Jessica answered cheerily. "If," she added less confidently, "I can get it to school without totally destroying it. It's really too big to carry so far."

"Is that a hint that you want a ride today?" Mr. Wakefield stood up, folded his newspaper, and put it into his briefcase. "If it is, the train leaves right now."

Jessica scampered to get her books and coat. "Gee, Liz," she said in a voice that sounded genuinely sorry, "I was counting on walking with you and Brooke. But I guess my schoolwork has to come first." Before Elizabeth could say a word, Jessica had kissed her mother and was out the door, following her father to the car. In dismay, Elizabeth tagged behind and watched her twin wave gaily. "See you in school, big sister!"

Behind her, Elizabeth heard loud applause.

She turned to find Steven clapping his hands above his empty plate. "What a performance," he cheered. "Jessica's going to win an Academy Award one of these days!"

Elizabeth smiled in spite of herself. "Well," she told him, "she didn't have me fooled for one minute."

Now it was time for Mrs. Wakefield to leave. Scooping up her coat and briefcase, she walked over to Elizabeth and tilted her chin up for a kiss. "I know Brooke Dennis didn't seem like the most charming girl in the world, dear. But my bet is you're just the person who can help get that chip off her shoulder."

"Elizabeth might be able to knock the chip off Brooke's shoulder," mused Steven, "but I just wonder how she's going to get Brooke's swelled head down to size."

"If anyone can do it, Elizabeth can." Her mother tousled Steven's wavy brown hair affectionately and then hurried out the door. "Don't forget to lock up, you two," she called over her shoulder.

Elizabeth was glad her mother had so much confidence in her. But, as she said goodbye to Steven and headed for Brooke's house, she didn't feel too confident herself. She felt even more doubtful when she spotted Brooke waiting impatiently by the front door. "What took you so long?" she asked as soon as Elizabeth reached her. "Walking that dilapidated dog?"

"No. You've got me confused with Jessica. She got a ride to school with my dad. We'll see her later."

"I can hardly wait." Brooke turned on her heel, her long brown hair fluttering behind her. She was dressed very properly again, Elizabeth noticed. Her green blouse and skirt were perfectly matched with a necklace of emerald beads and small lime-colored earrings.

Elizabeth started to walk beside Brooke. "Have you gotten your class schedule yet?" Elizabeth asked, trying to be friendly.

"No."

"Do you know who your homeroom teacher is?"

"No, and I don't care, either."

Elizabeth had known that the walk to school would be unpleasant, but this was even worse than she'd feared. Still, she was determined not to get upset with Brooke. "I just thought we might have some classes together," Elizabeth pressed on. "And, if you're interested in working on the sixth grade newspaper, we can always use writers."

"Well, don't worry. I have better things to do with my time than write for some dumb kids' paper."

At this point, the only thing keeping Elizabeth from snapping was that she didn't want to disappoint her mother. Besides, Mr. Bowman had wanted a story about Brooke for the *Sixers*. *Maybe if I change the subject* . . . thought Elizabeth. "Brooke, I know you must have led a pretty exciting life with such an important father," she said. "What was it like in Hollywood?"

Brooke stopped her brisk walk and faced Elizabeth. "Look," she said with the same scowl on her face Elizabeth remembered from the night before. "I don't want to walk to school with *you* any more than you want to walk with *me*. So let's make this as painless as possible and cut out the twenty-questions routine. OK?"

Brooke didn't need to ask twice. Elizabeth was only too glad to walk the rest of the way in silence. In fact, she would have given anything to be walking beside anyone but Disgusting Dennis.

Three

◇

By the time the two girls arrived at the front steps of Sweet Valley Middle School, Elizabeth was tired and angry. Usually, she began the school day feeling full of energy and eager to talk to her friends. Today, she wished she could hide in a hole rather than introduce Brooke Dennis to her friends. Unfortunately, two of her best friends met them at the door.

Amy Sutton and Julie Porter worked on the paper with Elizabeth. Amy, tall and tomboyish, was Elizabeth's favorite friend at school. Though Jessica sometimes made fun of Amy for being shy and awkward, Elizabeth loved her friend's quiet sense of humor. Julie was a lot like Elizabeth—a pretty, friendly girl who went her own way.

"Hi, Elizabeth." Julie's eyes were blazing with excitement. "Guess which three super reporters have a special meeting with Mr. Bowman after school today?"

"You mean he likes our idea to do record reviews?" Elizabeth was so glad their plans for a new music column had been approved that she almost forgot about Brooke. Then the first bell rang, and students began filing past them. Suddenly she remembered she hadn't introduced her neighbor to the two girls.

"Amy and Julie, we've got someone new in our class. This is Brooke Dennis. She just moved into our neighborhood with her father." Elizabeth held her breath as she turned toward the quiet girl beside her. "Brooke, these are two of my friends, Amy Sutton and Julie Porter."

"Listen," Brooke told Elizabeth and her two friends, "I think it's just great that the three of you are such terrific friends." She looked briefly at Amy and Julie, then turned back to Elizabeth. "But if you're asking me to join your happy little family, you can forget it right now."

Amy's pale blue eyes shut and then opened again. She stared at the pretty new girl as if she couldn't believe what she'd heard. Julie, however, reacted quickly. "Actually," she told Brooke, "nobody asked you. Elizabeth was just trying to be polite—something you wouldn't know much about."

"I know one thing," Brooke responded coldly as the last bell rang. "I don't intend to be around here long enough to get to know any of you. And that's a loss I can live with," she added sourly.

Elizabeth's patience had just about run out,

but she decided to see her new neighbor to her homeroom. As she raced to her first class, Elizabeth hoped like mad that the two of them would not end up in many of the same classes. She wanted to enjoy the rest of the day!

It was with real relief that she learned Brooke had been assigned to another sixth grade homeroom. At least that meant that she and Jessica wouldn't have to deal with their neighbor first thing in the morning. Unfortunately, Brooke was scheduled for social studies with Jessica. Elizabeth knew that Mrs. Arnette's class was already her twin's least favorite time of the day. She hated to think what would happen when Jessica found out.

Elizabeth had every reason to worry. The minute Jessica took her seat in Mrs. Arnette's class and found Brooke beside her, the trouble started.

"So which Bobbsey Twin are you?" asked Brooke. "As if I cared," she added snidely.

"I'm Jessica."

"Oh, yes. The one with the tummy ache. Did Mommy make it all better?"

Jessica was not nearly as good as her twin at controlling her temper. "Yes," she snapped back. "My stomachache's gone. But with you around, now I have a pain in the neck."

Fortunately, Brooke didn't have time to answer. Mrs. Arnette rose from her desk to call roll. One by one, the students answered to their names. Just as she reached the P's, Caroline Pearce, whose desk was at the front of the room, let out an earsplitting shriek and clapped a hand over her cheek.

"For heaven's sake, Caroline, dear. What is the matter?" Mrs. Arnette rushed to the embarrassed girl's side and began examining her face.

Jessica and most of the other students had seen Charlie Cashman aim the rubber band toward the first row. Always ready to play a trick, Charlie had pulled back the elastic as if he were drawing a bow. Then he let fly and pounded his chest with a fist. Many members of the class started to laugh. Charlie, who loved to get a reaction, was bowing from the waist at his desk.

"I'll tell you what's the matter," Brooke announced from her seat beside Jessica. "That boy there shot a rubber band." She pointed a finger at Charlie, who turned in surprise to face his strange accuser. "And," she added, glaring at Jessica, "a lot of people in this class think it was pretty funny."

The whole room was suddenly dead silent. Even Mrs. Arnette seemed shocked. Caroline Pearce, who should have been angriest of all at Charlie, broke the silence by whispering loudly to the girl beside her. "Just what we need in this class—an FBI informer!"

Everyone had heard Caroline's loud complaint, and now the entire class burst out laughing. And the entire class, with one exception, thought tattletales were the lowest form of humanity. The one exception, of course, was Brooke Dennis. She sat stiffly in her seat and nodded with approval when Mrs. Arnette told Charlie he'd have to stay after school and warned the rest of the class they had better settle down unless they wanted to join him.

Brooke's popularity with her new classmates didn't improve as the day wore on. By the time English began, word about the rubber band incident had gotten around to most of the students in Mr. Bowman's room. Jessica, minus her book report, was in no mood for another class with Brooke. Strolling into class just as the final bell sounded, she was relieved to find she was seated far away from her neighbor. "Thank goodness," she confided to her best friend, Lila Fowler, "we've got four rows between us and Miss Priss."

Lila was a Unicorn and a member of the Boosters. She, too, had had more than enough of Brooke's rudeness. "Do you know that just now in the hall she suggested that I was slowing her down because I wasn't walking fast enough!" She tossed her shoulder-length hair and fingered the strand of pearls that looped across her pink sweater. "As if I twisted my ankle on purpose! As if I wanted to miss cheering at the game tonight."

Jessica saw the scorn in her friend's angry eyes. If looks could kill, she thought, Brooke Dennis would have crumpled over at her desk. "Don't worry about Disgusting Dennis," she whispered as Mr. Bowman took roll. "I have a feeling we can make her sorry she ever came to this school."

Lila, who liked a good scheme as much as Jessica, smiled with anticipation. "I love the way your mind works, Jessica. I'm willing to do my part, as long as it's nasty!"

Both girls were so busy giggling that they almost missed the best news of the day. Instead of asking students to read their book reports, Mr. Bowman told his class they could spend the period finishing their posters for the book fair. Jessica was delighted. Not only could she put off her report another day, but she would do something she enjoyed. Her work on the poster had been fun, and she looked forward to all the compliments she'd get as soon as the class saw it.

Sure enough, everyone began to crowd around the big sheet. "That's about the most professional job I've ever seen," Charlie Cashman said admiringly, "even if mine *is* more colorful." He unrolled his poster and placed it on the table beside Jessica's. The students around them shook with laughter as they saw the bright green baggy pants and the polka-dot hat he'd painted on the boy in his picture.

"*Tom Sawyer* isn't about a clown!" joked Jerry McAllister.

"I know," Charlie admitted. "But I figured Mark Twain wouldn't mind me dressing up his hero a little bit. After all, how can an ordinary guy compete against that cute Nancy Drew?"

"It doesn't seem like there's much competition, anyway," Jerry said, glancing at Jessica's poster.

"It doesn't seem like there's much work being done, either." Mr. Bowman was smiling, but he clearly meant business. Quickly, the group around Jerry and Jessica broke up. Everyone concentrated on finishing the work for Friday's book fair.

"Since you're new in class," the English teacher told Brooke, "I don't think there will be time for you to do a poster of your own." He put an arm on Brooke's shoulder and steered her toward Jessica and Lila, who were working side by

side. "Why don't you help Lila with her project on
Charlotte's Web?"

Jessica looked at her friend. Lila was as stiff as
a board, and her mouth was frozen into a straight
line.

Brooke waited until Mr. Bowman had walked
to the other side of the room before glancing at
Lila's poster. "That looks more like a traffic jam
than a spider's web," she said coolly, studying the
tangled lines Lila had painted in blue underneath
the book's title.

"Well, I'm not surprised that you're an expert
on bugs," Lila snapped. She dipped her brush into
the blue paint and handed it to Brooke. "Since you
could do so much better, why don't you just take
over?"

"Sure. Why not?" Brooke grabbed the brush
and pushed Lila aside. She guided the brush over
the poster in a series of sharp, jagged lines. She
was dipping her brush into the jar for the second
time, when she accidentally knocked over the jar
with the brush. Before anyone realized it, the blue
paint had poured in a shiny stream over the desk
and across Jessica's poster. In seconds all the carefully traced adventures of Nancy Drew were covered with a blue streak.

Jessica was so stunned that she didn't make a
sound. She stood over her ruined project with a
look of horror on her face. Huge tears began to
form in the corners of her blue-green eyes.

"How could you?" Lila shouted at Brooke.
"Do you know how much work went into that
poster?" She stood opposite Brooke, her hands on
her hips. "What's the matter with you, anyway?

You've done nothing but make everyone miserable since you got here!"

Mr. Bowman joined the girls as soon as he heard Lila yelling. "What's the trouble over here?" he asked.

Jessica shook her head and stared at her ruined poster. "Brooke knocked the paint over," she told him. "My Nancy Drew project is . . . is . . ." She felt tears coming and couldn't finish her sentence.

Instead of apologizing, Brooke stunned Jessica by insisting angrily, "I did not."

Lila and Jessica stared at each other in disbelief. It was bad enough that Brooke had destroyed the poster, but for her to deny it was just too much! "Then how do you explain the paint all over Jessica's work?" Lila demanded.

"You know very well how it got there." Brooke turned calmly to face the teacher. "Mr. Bowman, Lila knocked my elbow just as I was helping her finish the web. She was standing behind me, and I guess she didn't like the way I was painting."

"What?" Lila's face was dark with rage. "I never even touched you!" She glared at the tall girl with more hatred than Jessica had ever seen. "I'd be afraid of catching something!"

"Now, girls," cautioned Mr. Bowman, "I wouldn't want to keep you both after school. The important thing is not who's to blame, but how we can help Jessica." He waved his hand toward the paint, which by now had run across the desk and onto the floor.

"But, Mr. Bowman," Lila stammered, trying

to explain. "I didn't have anything to do with it. I . . ."

"Everybody makes mistakes," Brooke told her. "Too bad some of us can't admit it."

"Never mind." Mr. Bowman handed a damp rag to Lila and a mop to Brooke. "You're *both* on clean-up duty until this mess is mopped up."

Four

Even though Lila usually insisted on eating lunch at the Unicorn table, Jessica waved as soon as she saw her sister and Amy at the back of the cafeteria. "Come on," she urged her friend. "Let's sit with Elizabeth so I can fill her in." Balancing a mini-pizza on her tray, she raced across the room to share her disappointment with the one person who always understood how she felt.

Elizabeth knew right away that something was bothering her twin. "You look terrible, Jess. What's the matter?"

"Only everything, Liz. Only my whole life is ruined. And it's all because of that new girl. I wish she and her father would pack their bags and move to Alaska."

"Yeah," added Lila, joining them. "Or maybe to the North Pole."

When Elizabeth heard about the accident, she felt awful. She knew how much Jessica had wanted to win the poster contest. Mr. Bowman and the book fair committee had decided to award a Kendall's gift certificate as well as a book club membership this year. Jessica had already picked out a jumpsuit at her favorite department store!

"Gosh, Jess. I just know you would have won," said Elizabeth. "Are you sure you can't fix your project?"

"If Jessica can fix *that* mess," commented Lila, "she could turn Brooke Dennis into Snow White!"

"I'm afraid it's true, Liz." Jessica sighed and used her napkin to wipe a tear from her eye. "My poster looks like it's advertising a brand-new Nancy Drew mystery, *The Case of the Blue Smear!*"

"At least it was an accident," said Amy. "I mean it's not as if she did it on purpose." Like Elizabeth, Amy didn't hurry to judge others harshly. "Maybe she was really trying to help."

"With that kind of help," Lila told the girls, "Brooke is just about the last person in the world anybody would want for a friend. Besides," she added, lowering her voice to a whisper, "I wouldn't be a bit surprised if she knew exactly what she was doing."

"What?" Even Jessica couldn't believe what Lila was suggesting.

"You should have seen Brooke's face when Mr. Bowman told you what a great job you'd done. She looked incredibly jealous!"

"Lila, do you think Brooke ruined my sister's poster on purpose?"

But Lila had no time to answer Elizabeth's

question. A hush fell over the table as Jessica pointed to the front of the room. Brooke Dennis was storming away from the cafeteria line, and her face was bright red.

"Guess what just happened?" Caroline Pearce raced to the table and barely waited for an answer to her question. "Brooke just told off Bruce Patman!"

"You've got to be kidding!" Jessica knew that hardly anyone ever argued with Bruce. His father was one of the wealthiest men in Sweet Valley. Spoiled, handsome Bruce could always get his way—and he had plenty of friends to stick up for him!

"You should have heard her!" Caroline's face was flushed with excitement. There was nothing she liked better than a good story. This was the best she'd had to tell in a long, long time. "She asked him who he thought he was for getting into line ahead of her, and then she called him a jerk." Caroline paused while everyone turned back to watch the tall, good-looking boy amble over to a seat at a nearby table.

"And she mentioned you, too, Jessica." Caroline smiled at both twins, relishing their surprise. "She said that between Bruce and 'crybaby Wakefield' she'd had enough of this school!"

"How can she talk that way about Jessica?" Elizabeth fumed. "If that girl knew what was good for her, she'd . . ."

Elizabeth stopped suddenly, staring in disbelief as Brooke left the lunch line and walked toward their table. As naturally as if she had been invited, Brooke put her tray in front of the empty seat by Lila.

"Wait a minute. You can't sit here," said Amy.

"And why, may I ask, *can't* I sit here? This *is* a public school isn't it? Or did you guys pay for this table?"

"Look, there are plenty of other tables," suggested Lila. "Go ruin someone else's day. This seat's taken."

"That's funny." Brooke glared at the fifth chair. "It looks pretty empty to me."

"Well, it's not," said Elizabeth, trying to hold her temper. "We're saving it."

"That's right," Lila agreed suddenly. "It's reserved."

"Yes!" Suddenly Jessica came alive. She had come up with the perfect scheme. "That seat's saved for my sister."

"Your what?" For the first time, Brooke looked confused. "What do you mean? Your sister's right here."

"My other sister. Didn't you know? We're triplets. That seat's saved for Jennifer."

Elizabeth didn't like to lie. But for once, she felt that someone actually deserved to be on the wrong end of one of Jessica's crazy schemes. Trying to keep from laughing, she nodded vigorously. "That's right," she told Brooke, "Jennifer will be here any minute. Isn't that so, Amy?"

"Sure," Amy told Brooke. "She'll be here. It's just that Jennifer's always late."

"I don't know about you all, but I'm going for more pizza." Jessica slipped out of her place and ran toward the food line.

Brooke didn't even watch her go. She was too interested in getting to the bottom of things. "And just where was Jennifer last night?" she asked Elizabeth.

"She and Jessica both had the same stomach-ache," Elizabeth assured Brooke. "Besides," she added smiling, "she hates lemon meringue pie."

"That's right, I do. Hi, everybody. Thanks for saving my place."

Everyone looked up in amazement. There was Jessica—or was it? Elizabeth noticed that her sister had put on the blue cardigan she kept in her locker. She'd also changed her hair by pinning a blue bow behind one ear. Jessica's voice had changed, too. It was small and whispery, not at all like her usual confident tone.

"Hi, Jennifer," said Lila, catching on right away. "Wait till you hear what happened in English class." She glared pointedly at Brooke.

The others joined in, and soon were chatting with "Jennifer" as if she had always been a member of their group. "By the way, Jen," Elizabeth announced, "this is Brooke Dennis. You know, the guest you missed last night." Jessica turned to Brooke. "Oh, yes," she whispered in her soft voice. "I'm *so* glad to meet you, Brooke. I just *know* we're going to be great friends."

"Not as long as you hang around with this crowd," Brooke told her. Jennifer turned to Brooke with a knowing smile. Brooke picked up her tray and stalked off to another table. Behind her the four girls collapsed into giggles.

"Boy," Lila told the twins when she finally stopped laughing, "you two—or should I say three?—have really started something."

"You bet we have," promised Jessica, grinning

triumphantly at her sister. "And we're just the ones who can finish it, too! Wait till you see how nice Jennifer is going to be to Brooke, even if it kills her. Pretty soon she's going to have Disgusting Dennis eating right out of her hand."

"What a great idea!" Lila grinned. "Once Brooke trusts Jennifer, we can really have some fun!!" She stood up, her uneaten pizza still on her tray. "But we have to move fast," she reminded them. "We've got to spread the word before Brooke finds out Jennifer doesn't really exist!"

"That's right," Amy agreed. "I'll tell everyone in my math class all about the Wakefield triplets. The rest of you, spread the word next period."

The girls decided to make sure that all the kids in the sixth grade would keep this prank a secret. They were sure everyone would cooperate, since Brooke had snubbed every single person who tried to be nice to her. Getting back at Disgusting Dennis was going to be a class project!

"Just remember," Jessica cautioned them, "Jennifer always wears a bow and talks in a whisper. Make sure everyone is in on it."

And everyone was. For the rest of the day, no matter what classroom she entered, as long as she was wearing the tiny bow, Jessica was greeted as Jennifer. Lila had passed the word to the rest of the Unicorns, so that even seventh graders like Kimberly Haver and eighth graders like Janet Howell, the Unicorns' president, went along.

"Hi, Jennifer," Janet sang out as Brooke and Jessica passed her in the hall. "Tell Jessica there's a club meeting after school today."

"Thank goodness," Brooke confided to Jennifer. "I'm glad it's going to be just you on the walk home today. No offense, Jennifer, but I don't like Jessica one bit. In fact, you're about the only person in this whole school I'd consider talking to."

It was true. Jessica had been so busy trying to fool Brooke that she'd ignored all the nasty things her neighbor said and did. Instead, she'd stuck to the new girl's side all afternoon, pretending to enjoy being with her. Now Brooke thought she'd found someone to listen to her selfish complaints.

"I don't understand the way everybody fusses over Jessica," Brooke was telling her now. "It was enough to make me sick. What's she got anyway?"

"I don't know," Jessica answered quickly, trying to stifle a laugh. "I've never understood all that sports and cheerleading stuff Jessica likes."

"Me neither. Hey, do you want to go see a movie tonight?"

"I—I—can't," Jessica stammered. "I'm supposed to go to the basketball game."

"I thought you said you hate sports!" Brooke challenged her new friend.

"No. It's not that," Jessica covered her mistake quickly. "It's just that I always watch Jessica cheer. She needs me there. She can't do a thing without me."

"Well, if you like her better than me . . ."

"It's not that." Jessica felt desperate. She didn't want to lose Brooke's trust. "Hey, why don't you come to the game *with* me?" she suggested. "We'll sit through the whole boring thing together."

"OK, I guess. See you after school."

Jessica watched Brooke wave and head for her last class. What on earth was she going to do now, Jessica wondered. She had a Unicorn meeting after school, when she was supposed to be walking home with Brooke. And on top of that, she'd promised to take Brooke to watch herself cheer!

"Hi, Jennifer, what's up?" Elizabeth teased as she walked up to her twin. But Jessica didn't need teasing. She needed help. She tore the blue bow from her hair.

"It's *me*, Liz. Remember, your one and only sister?"

"Oh, yes." Elizabeth grinned. "The budding actress. The one with the great big stomachaches and the heavy, heavy posters."

"Listen, big sister. This is no time for kidding around. We're in serious trouble. I've got a Unicorn meeting, so Jennifer can't walk Brooke home. I mean *this* Jennifer can't."

"Jessica Wakefield, don't you dare even suggest it for one minute," Elizabeth protested, knowing what her twin was about to ask. "I'm already into this mess as deep as I want to go."

"Oh, Liz, come on. You dislike Brooke as much as I do. Besides, if you do me this one special favor, I'll never ever ask you to do anything else for me as long as I live."

"Or until you need an understudy again." Elizabeth couldn't contain her smile. "I have to admit, Jess. This scheme of yours is absolutely brilliant."

"Then you'll walk Brooke home?"

"Sure," agreed Elizabeth. "But you better fill me in on what Jennifer and Brooke talked about today. It sounds as if you two got pretty chummy."

As they walked to their last class, Jessica brought her twin up to date. Elizabeth took the blue bow and hid it in her notebook. Jessica gave her the cardigan and then hurried down the hall.

Watching her sister race off, Elizabeth wondered what Jessica had gotten them both into. It was one thing to be triplets for an afternoon, but how long could they keep it up? Wouldn't Brooke begin to wonder why she never saw Elizabeth, Jessica, and Jennifer all together? And what would happen when Brooke discovered what a fool they had made of her? Aside from these questions, something else kept bothering her all through history class. Elizabeth couldn't help wondering: Was anybody really nasty enough to deserve such a dirty trick?

Five

◇

After class, Elizabeth and Brooke started home.
They were down the steps and passing the teachers' parking lot when Amy caught up with them.
Panting and out of breath, she signaled for them to
stop.

"Jennifer, have you seen Elizabeth?" Amy
wore a strange, frantic expression. "Mr. Bowman
is looking for her everywhere. We've got a meeting
for the newspaper. Do you think she forgot?"

"Uh—yes." Elizabeth looked at Brooke and
added quickly, "I hope so anyway. I'm tired of
hearing about that dumb paper."

"Dumb is right," Brooke told her. "She talks
about that paper as if it were *The New York Times*
instead of a silly little typed-up rag."

Amy looked at Elizabeth meaningfully. "Mr.
Bowman told me he'd look for Elizabeth outside

while I scouted out the gym. He thought maybe she was trying to get a story on the game tonight."

Brooke seemed confused. "Well, if Mr. Bowman sent you to look for Elizabeth in the gym, what are you doing out here? There aren't any basketball fans here, right, Jennifer?"

Now Elizabeth understood why Amy had rushed after them. It would ruin all their plans if Mr. Bowman cornered Jennifer now. But it was too late. Just behind them, running at a leisurely athletic clip, was the English teacher. As he waved and joined them, Elizabeth's heart sank.

"I'm glad Amy caught up with you, Elizabeth." Mr. Bowman was carrying back issues of *The Sweet Valley Sixers* under his arm. "We've got a lot of ground to cover if you want to start a music column."

Before Brooke or Elizabeth could say a word, Amy took control. "Sorry, Mr. Bowman. But I got the wrong Wakefield. These look-alikes always fool me."

"You mean we still have to nail down Elizabeth? I thought I finally had you girls sorted out!" Mr. Bowman laughed and turned back toward the gym with Amy. "See you tomorrow, Brooke. You too, Jessica."

"It's amazing." Brooke was shaking her head beside Elizabeth as the two continued home. "He still hasn't got you right. I guess it happens all the time, huh?"

"It sure does." Elizabeth breathed a sigh of relief and felt grateful Amy had gotten to them in time. "Being a triplet means you never know *who* someone thinks you are." *Sometimes,* she thought, *you're not even sure yourself!*

It wasn't until after dinner that Jessica broke the bad news. That afternoon's close calls were just the beginning. Since Jennifer had already agreed to go with Brooke to the game, someone had to play Jennifer while Jessica cheered. The someone who was selected was *not* happy about it.

"What do you mean I have to help you out?" cried Elizabeth. "What happened to your never asking me for another favor for as long as you live?"

Jessica put both hands on her twin's shoulders and gazed soulfully into Elizabeth's eyes. "Oh, Liz. You know I'd never ask you to do anything so risky unless my life depended on it. Brooke hates me so much. If she found out now how we'd been fooling her, I just don't know what she'd do!"

"It would probably be the best thing for all of us if Brooke found out what we were up to. I had to phone Mr. Bowman after school and make up some ridiculous reason for not going to the newspaper meeting. All I could think of was that I felt sick. And, little sister, that wasn't exactly a lie!"

Jessica knew that Elizabeth hated to deceive people. While she herself didn't see anything wrong with an occasional fib, her twin liked to be honest all the time. "Don't worry, Liz. I promise it won't be for much longer. Lila and I are going to come up with a terrific plan to put Brooke in her place once and for all." Her blue-green eyes narrowed as she thought about how sorry Brooke Dennis was going to be that she had ever moved to Sweet Valley.

"If it weren't for the way she's treated you, Jess, I wouldn't have anything to do with your schemes. But every time I remember how she's picked on you and the way she acted with Mom and Dad I get angry all over again."

Jessica gave Elizabeth a big hug. "I *knew* you'd help. You're the best triplet I ever had, Liz!" Suddenly she was sorting through the clothes in her sister's closet. "Now, let's see if we can find the perfect outfit for Jennifer tonight."

Elizabeth, who was used to her sister's borrowing every piece of clothing she owned, laughed. "And why can't Jennifer wear something of *yours* to the game?"

"Oh, Elizabeth." Jessica continued sorting through the dresses and skirts hanging in the closet. "We don't want Jennifer to wear anything too smart. She should be more like you. You know, not really caring how she looks."

"Thanks a lot!"

Jessica put Elizabeth's gray jumper back on the rack with the other outfits and turned to her sister. "You know what I mean," she said in a serious tone. "You're good at so many things, Liz. You're a terrific writer, a great dancer, and you're just about the smartest girl in our class." She looked at Elizabeth with open admiration. "I'm different. Everyone knows it." Her long lashes lowered, and she smiled almost shyly at her twin. "I could never be as bright, talented, or sweet as you, Liz. What else have I got to care about but being popular and looking good?"

Elizabeth stared at her sister. "You're every bit as smart and talented as I am, Jessica Wakefield!" she exclaimed. "If you didn't spend so much time on cheerleading, you'd be the best student in Madame André's ballet class. And if you weren't so busy with Unicorn meetings, you could do just as well as I do in school."

"Maybe better!" Jessica laughed and hugged Elizabeth again. "Thanks for not letting me feel sorry for myself, Lizzie. I guess I'm more the goof-off type than the homework type."

"Speaking of types," Elizabeth added thoughtfully. "Just exactly what type is Jennifer?"

"You know, I invented Jennifer so fast, I didn't have time to figure out what she's like."

"Neither did I. As far as I can see, though, she's a big hit with Brooke."

"She sure is," agreed Jessica. "Disgusting Dennis is crazy about her. I wonder why."

"Well, she's got everything going for her, as far as Brooke's concerned."

"Why?" Jessica looked confused. "What do you mean?"

"Simple," announced Elizabeth grinning. "She's not like either of *us*!"

"Right. She's not much fun at all, so she's a perfect match for Disgusting Dennis. And," Jessica announced, "if Jennifer's not like either of us, she shouldn't dress like either of us. Maybe we should use some of Steven's clothes for Jennifer. What do you say?"

"Well, it will be different," Elizabeth said, picturing herself strolling beside Brooke in one of Steven's huge Rugby jerseys. "Let's do it!"

And they did. Steven disliked Brooke as much as the twins and agreed readily. In fact, he loved being part of their plan. "But remember," he warned the twins, "if Mom finds out any of this, I never heard about it." He piled three sweaters and several Rugby shirts into Jessica's arms. "After all, this is her big client's daughter you're tricking. I don't mind your pulling the wool over Brooke's eyes, but I just don't want Mom to find out I said it was okay to use my sweaters!"

The gymnasium was packed with fans when Brooke and "Jennifer" arrived for the basketball game. The girls scrambled up the bleachers, tripping over legs and coats. They reached what seemed like the last two seats in the gym. "Boy," Brooke told her new friend, "I can't believe so many kids like this stupid game."

Elizabeth, who really loved to watch Jessica cheer, tried to pretend she felt the same way Brooke did. "I know," she observed, scanning the rows ahead of them. "These kids could be doing a lot better things with their time than watching ten guys fight over a ball."

"Wow!" Brooke sounded amused. "You know pretty much about basketball, don't you? I don't even know how many players make up a team." As the referee blew his whistle for the opening jump, she looked at Jennifer, then turned her attention to the gym floor.

"Elizabeth and Jessica keep pounding it into

my head. They really like this stupid game." Elizabeth felt warm in the crowded room and began wriggling out of her jacket. "Besides, our dad takes us to ball games all the time."

Brooke watched the play for a minute more before answering her friend. "In a way, Jennifer," she told Elizabeth, "you're pretty lucky. My dad doesn't take me anywhere much. I mean all he cares about are movies."

Elizabeth suddenly heard the tiny, nagging voice of her conscience again. Maybe Brooke wasn't as tough as she wanted everyone to think she was. Maybe this whole scheme wasn't such a great idea after all. The voice got even louder when Brooke looked at the outfit Elizabeth was wearing.

"Hey, you look cute, Jen."

Elizabeth could hardly believe the kind, friendly expression on her neighbor's face. "Thanks, Brooke," she said, amazed at the compliment. "I sure didn't expect you, of all people, to like the way I dress."

"Oh, you mean because of *my* clothes? I didn't even get to pick them out. Dad hired some woman to select a whole school wardrobe for me. Everything she chose is either too tight or too hot. I've tried to tell Dad, but he's always got his nose buried in some script." She looked longingly at Elizabeth's loose, flowing shirt. "I'd give anything to have an outfit like yours."

Elizabeth was feeling worse and worse. She began to hope they wouldn't have to talk with anyone from school. Perhaps they could just watch the game and hurry home. She didn't find fooling Brooke as much fun as she and Jessica had planned. Unfortunately, everyone else still thought tricking Brooke was a terrific idea. Especially Lila Fowler. The girls had only been seated a few minutes, when Lila worked her way toward the top row to join them.

"Hi, Jennifer," she said loudly, squeezing in beside Elizabeth. "I hope you and your sisters haven't forgotten about my slumber party this weekend. *Everybody's* coming. I mean everybody who matters!" She glanced briefly at Brooke, who was dressed in a tangerine dress with a broad yellow-and-orange print belt. "Oh, Brooke. I'm sorry nobody told you about our quaint local customs. We don't usually require formal dress at sporting events."

"Look, Lila. This wasn't exactly my idea of a fun place to spend the evening." Brooke folded her arms, and the old, familiar scowl reappeared on her face. "I only came to keep Jennifer company."

"And *I* just came to watch Jessica cheer." Elizabeth was relieved to see the Booster squad run out onto the floor. "So if you two could postpone your argument till later, I'd appreciate it."

"Give me an S!" Jessica was standing in front of the squad with her hands on her hips.

"Give me an aspirin," Brooke said sarcastically. "I'm going to be sick."

"Give me a W!" Now all the Boosters had joined Jessica in a circle, kicking high with each letter they named.

"Give me an E-E-T!"

"Gosh," said Lila, gazing intently at each formation the girls performed. "I sure wish I hadn't twisted my ankle, or I'd be out there with them."

"What's stopping you?" asked Brooke. "They all cheer like they've got broken ankles."

Elizabeth didn't like what she was hearing. "Now wait a minute, Brooke. Jessica and the others put a lot of time and work into these routines."

"Look, Jennifer." Brooke turned suddenly to Elizabeth. "I know Jessica is your sister and everyone loves her to death, but frankly, I couldn't care less." The expression in her brown eyes was halfway between tears and anger. "I thought you and I were friends, but if you're always going to take sides with that shallow, spoiled little—"

"They scored!" Lila was on her feet and yelling with everyone else in the gym. Elizabeth, standing now with the crowd, felt the anger rush to her cheeks. How could anyone talk about Jessica that way?

As the crowd seated itself, the cheerleaders counted off the points of the first score. "One," they all yelled as Jessica executed a perfect cartwheel. "Two," everyone cheered, and Jessica once more began a cartwheel. But this time something went wrong. Instead of landing upright, Jessica kept turning and landed in an awkward heap on the floor.

"Jess!" Elizabeth was on her feet, trying to make her way down to the bottom of the stands. She could see Jessica was already picking herself up and getting in line for the next cheer, but she also knew how embarrassed and hurt her twin must feel. She wanted to watch the rest of the game from right up front, where Jessica would know she was there for her.

But Brooke had other ideas. "She's all right. Don't worry about her," she urged.

Elizabeth stopped and stared up at Brooke. She was smiling—a big, broad smile that made it clear she had actually enjoyed watching Jessica fall. Now there was no more small voice telling Elizabeth it was wrong to trick Brooke Dennis. For one second, Elizabeth wanted to race back up the bleachers and show Brooke just how it felt to fall flat on your face in front of hundreds of people.

But she stopped herself. Or rather Lila stopped her. Jessica's friend had followed Elizabeth to help, but now she grabbed Elizabeth's elbow and pulled her down on a seat beside her. "Don't let her spoil our plan, Elizabeth," she whispered. "That would be letting her off too easy."

Elizabeth took a deep breath and counted to ten. Lila, of course, was right. For Jessica's sake, "Jennifer" would have to go on liking Brooke, even though everyone else hated her. She might not know it yet, Elizabeth promised herself as she returned to her old seat, but Brooke was sure going to find out that no one could ever come between the Wakefield twins!

Six

◇

Both Elizabeth and Jessica were relieved when Friday came and Brooke's father took her to a Hollywood screening for the weekend. "Thank goodness!" Elizabeth sighed. "Two whole days of just being me—if I can remember how!"

"This triplets business has me dizzy, too," Jessica said with a laugh. "I don't know who worked harder after school today—you, decorating for the book fair or me, playing Jennifer on the walk home!"

Elizabeth nodded, remembering how she'd worked all that afternoon with Amy and the school fair committee, cutting paper streamers and lettering signs. They had turned each classroom into a different book. A title was displayed on each door and student reports and projects were featured inside. Elizabeth's heart, though, hadn't been in her work. She had spent most of the time thinking how unfair it was that someone besides Jessica would receive the poster prize on Monday.

Jessica's pink-and-white bedroom was a mess. Ned Wakefield had promised his family dinner out, and Jessica had strewn clothes everywhere, looking for just the right outfit. "What on earth did you and Brooke talk about when you were Jennifer at lunch today?" she asked. "On the way home, Disgusting asked me if I remembered the promise I'd made her. How could you promise that monster anything, Liz?"

"Promise?" Elizabeth looked confused. She remembered playing Jennifer at lunch that day, but she was sure she hadn't promised Brooke anything at all. "We just talked about school, and I let her tell me how she hated everyone and everything about Sweet Valley. You know, the usual."

Jessica smiled. "Yep. The old Dennis charm. And I'll bet I know who's at the head of her hate list, too!"

Elizabeth smiled. "A certain Jessica Wakefield's name did come up. But you weren't at the top of the list today, Jess. Brooke saved her best comments for Lila. It seems she's tired of listening to all the excitement over Lila's birthday slumber party tomorrow."

"Uh-oh. I guess the wicked witch is mad we didn't invite her, huh?"

Elizabeth remembered the look of scorn on Brooke's face. She was criticizing the "fuss" people made over birthdays. "She told me that no one ever asked to be born, and it didn't take any talent to get a year older. She said she didn't know why people gave themselves parties and she wouldn't go to one, even if she were invited."

"Well, tell Brooke not to worry. We're not about to throw her any surprise parties!"

Suddenly Elizabeth remembered. "That's it!" she told Jessica. "That's the promise Jennifer made Brooke!"

"What is?"

"Her birthday. It's next Monday, and I promised I wouldn't tell anyone." Elizabeth grinned as her sister fell to the floor in mock horror.

"Jennifer Wakefield! You mean you were going to keep it from me? My favorite person in the world world is having a birthday, and you weren't going to tell me!" Jessica rolled over and propped herself up on one elbow. "My other sister, Elizabeth, would never stoop so low."

"Oh, I don't know," said Elizabeth, joining the game. "Elizabeth promised you she'd chip in for your friend Lila's present tomorrow, and she just spent all her money treating Amy to a double banana split at Casey's."

Jessica stood up and walked to her closet. "So that's where you two were! Well, never mind. You already got Lila the best present of all." She began singing her favorite Johnny Buck song while she thumbed through all the outfits on her rack.

Elizabeth didn't feel the least guilty about spending the last of her allowance on Amy instead of Lila. It was Jessica who was Lila's friend, and Elizabeth was only going to the slumber party to please her twin. "What do you mean I already got Lila a present?" Elizabeth asked.

"Why, you just figured out when we're going to use Jennifer to get even with Brooke."

Elizabeth still didn't see. "When?"

"On her birthday, of course. It's perfect!" Jessica finally emerged from her closet, a triumphant gleam in her eyes and her favorite blue sweater in her hand. "Now, if we're going to the Beach View Inn, big sister, you'd better get dressed!"

The Beach View Inn was the Wakefields' favorite restaurant. Right on the beach overlooking the sea, it was romantic enough to please their mother, served steaks just the way their father liked them, and every order came with the twins' favorite nachos and dip. Since Steven was always hungry, he didn't care where they ate as long as his plate was full!

"How are things coming with Henry Dennis?" Mr. Wakefield asked his wife after the waiter had brought dessert. The twins held their breath. "And how are you two doing with that feisty daughter of his?"

"If feisty means gross and disgusting," Jessica told him, "nothing has changed at all, Dad. And everyone in school loves her just as much as we do."

Mrs. Wakefield looked concerned. "Jessica," she asked, "are your friends at school giving Brooke a hard time?"

"She's giving *them* a hard time," Jessica explained. "Honestly, Mom. She's just the meanest, nastiest person I've ever met."

"I can't understand it." Their mother stopped eating and looked out the picture window at a fishing boat coming into port. "Her father is one of the nicest, most agreeable clients I've ever had. How about you, Elizabeth? Have you given up on Brooke, too?"

Elizabeth hated to disappoint her mother, but she couldn't pretend to like someone so awful. "Let's put it this way, Mom. I'd rather not discuss Brooke while we're still eating."

"If talking about Brooke's making you sick, Liz, I think I could finish your dessert." Steven reached across the table and brandished a spoon over the whipped cream on Elizabeth's butter-scotch sundae.

"Oh, no you don't." Elizabeth defended her dessert with her fork, and she and Steven started a mock duel across the table.

"OK, musketeers," announced Mr. Wake-field. "I think it's time to call a truce and finish up." He looked at the twins with the serious ex-pression that Jessica always called his "courtroom face." "Girls, I know it isn't easy to be nice to someone who isn't nice to you. But, remember, you can't always tell why people are nasty. Brooke may not be as tough as she seems." He signaled the waiter to bring the check, then added, "So go easy on her, will you two? Everybody needs friends."

Before Elizabeth had a chance to feel guilty, her twin was racing ahead to a subject she consid-ered much more important. "You're right, Daddy," Jessica agreed. "Nothing's as important as friends, especially best friends. I just wish I could be with mine on her birthday tomorrow."

"What do you mean, Jessica? You've been talking about Lila's slumber party for a week. I thought you were counting on going."

"I was. Until I realized Liz and I can't afford to get her a birthday present." Jessica looked forlorn as she put her spoon into her empty dessert dish.

Mr. Wakefield's "courtroom face" disappeared completely as he burst out laughing. "Young lady, how did you do that? You took a lecture of mine and turned it into a request for an advance on your allowance." He reached into his pocket, paid the bill, and handed Jessica some money as well. "If I could learn some of your tricks, I'd never lose a case!"

"Now if I only had something to wear . . ." Jessica said suggestively.

"Don't push your luck, dear," Mr. Wakefield replied with a smile.

Lila's slumber party turned out to be the biggest birthday celebration Jessica or Elizabeth could remember. Nearly thirty girls and their sleeping bags, hair dryers, and stuffed animals were crowded into the Fowlers' rec-room. The girls gorged on pizza and popcorn and watched the latest videos on Lila's big screen television.

"Don't you youngsters ever get tired?" Mrs. Pervis asked, poking her head into the rec-room door shortly after eleven o'clock. The woman had helped take care of Lila ever since she was little, and the twins could tell that Lila's housekeeper spoiled her almost as much as her father did.

"Your father has asked me to make sure the noise level in this room stays below a sonic boom!"

"OK, Eva," Lila promised. "We'll be as quiet as mice."

"And about as neat, too." Mrs. Pervis laughed. "Just look at this mess. I think you girls got more food on the rug than you did in your mouths." She shook her head, smiling so broadly that everyone knew she wasn't angry at all. "Just one more movie, now, and then it's time for bed."

"What shall we watch, everyone?" Lila asked as the housekeeper quietly closed the door. "It's the last one, so I think we should take a vote."

"How about *Car Capers*?" suggested Ellen Riteman, a Unicorn who loved movie stars more than almost anything else. "I think Terry Landers is so dreamy in the chase scene."

Jessica, sitting cross-legged beside their hostess, frowned. "I wouldn't be caught dead watching a movie written by Brooke Dennis's father."

"That's right," agreed Mary Giaccio, a pretty seventh grade Unicorn with gray eyes and long blond hair. "Just think, every time we watch that movie, we're contributing to the care and feeding of Brooke Dennis."

"Yuck!" Tamara Chase snuggled deeper into her sleeping bag, and looked at Ellen reproachfully. "How could you?"

"Gosh," apologized Ellen, "I'm sorry. Still," she added, a dreamlike expression crossing her face, "Terry's so cute. . . ."

As Ellen spoke, pillows were hurled in her direction. Soon the room was filled with flying missiles and giggling girls. Finally, everyone collapsed, exhausted, on the floor.

Jessica helped dig Ellen out from a mountain of pillows. "Come on out of there now. We need you to stop mooning over movie stars and start figuring out how we can give Brooke the surprise birthday present she deserves."

"What do you mean?" Ellen sat up and pulled a feather out of her tangled hair.

"Well," confided Jessica, "it seems Brooke's birthday's coming up. Tell them, Liz."

"It's true," Elizabeth told the group. "Her birthday's on Monday."

"Who cares?" asked Tamara.

"Her best friend cares," Jessica declared. "Don't tell me you've forgotten that Brooke has one great, personal buddy at school."

They all smiled, remembering the last couple of days, when Jessica and Elizabeth had been masquerading as Jennifer.

"I almost slipped a couple of times," confessed Julie, who was sprawled on the floor next to Elizabeth. "I kept getting confused about who was who."

"Me, too." Mary, who had been looking through Lila's huge collection of videotapes, got up to join the others. "I just kept looking for that silly bow behind your ear. I never knew who'd be wearing it. But as soon as I saw it, I'd yell out, 'Hi, Jennifer.'"

"You think *you* were confused," Amy said with a laugh. "Elizabeth and I ran into Mr. Bowman while she was playing Jennifer."

"That's why we've got to move fast," Jessica told them. "Sooner or later, someone's bound to slip, or a teacher will catch on. So Liz and I thought Monday should be the day."

"The day for what?" Caroline Pearce, her long red hair clashing with her pink pajamas, asked, sitting up. She loved gossip and she loved schemes, and hated to be left out of either.

"That's what we've got to work out," Lila announced. "Brooke really trusts Jennifer now. Jennifer can get her to do anything we want. But, what?"

"Something excruciating," suggested Julie.

"Something revolting," added Caroline.

"Something humiliating," offered Lila, rolling over on her back to wave her freshly polished nails in the air. The polish was day-glo pink with silver sparkles, a present from Tamara. "But you've all forgotten something. Jennifer's not in any of Brooke's classes. How can we pull this off so everyone in school can be in on it?" Lila still remembered the way Brooke had blamed her for the accident with the poster. She wanted to make sure she was there when Brooke got what was coming to her.

"What about the book fair awards ceremony in the gym?" suggested Jessica.

"It's perfect!" Lila exclaimed. "Jessica, you're the only person I know who's so good at being bad. Now, the next question is, how do we punish that tattletale?"

"Whatever we do," Elizabeth told her, "I hope she falls flat on her face." She pictured the way

Brooke had smiled when Jessica fell in the gym. Now Brooke would know how it felt, she promised herself.

"How?" Everyone stopped to stare at the grim, determined look on Elizabeth's face. They were all surprised that gentle Elizabeth could dislike someone so much.

But Elizabeth was so furious at Brooke for her comments about Jessica that she hadn't thought out a careful plan. "I'm not really sure how," she confessed, "but I know who's going to help her fall."

"Her good friend Jennifer!" Jessica said.

"That's right. And then when she tries to tell the teachers who's responsible, they'll think she's crazy. How can you blame someone who doesn't even exist?"

"The perfect punishment for a tattletale!" Lila was delighted. "OK, everyone, Elizabeth's gotten us this far. Now it's up to the *real* schemers to take over. Let's all put our heads together and come up with something just right."

"You mean just *wrong*, don't you, Lila?" Janet Howell smiled at her cousin.

"You bet she does," said Jessica. Suddenly, her face lit up with a foxlike grin. "And I think I just thought of something so deliciously evil that we're going to need help from the boys."

"Tell! Tell!" Everyone was giggling and expectant.

"What kind of help?"

"What can the boys do?"

"Jerry McAllister takes shop, and Bruce Patman's father has the best-equipped basement workshop in town." Jessica looked at the ring of curious faces around her. "Don't you see?" she asked. "We're going to need expert advice if we're going to cut Brooke Dennis down to size!"

Seven

◇

Jessica's plan was simple, but it required fast action. "We'll have to talk to the boys tomorrow," she explained to Lila's guests. "If we want to give Brooke the special treatment she deserves on Monday, Jerry and Bruce will have to start work on a collapsible chair right away."

"A collapsible chair?" Elizabeth couldn't picture what her sister had in mind.

"Sure. Brooke's friend, Jennifer, is going to save her a *very special* seat for the book fair assembly. It'll be right up front, where everyone can watch when Disgusting Dennis falls right through her chair."

"Gosh," said Mary Giaccio admiringly. "I would never have thought of that."

"Do you think Jerry can really do it?" Lila asked.

"You bet he can!" Amy exclaimed. "I've seen some of the stuff he built in shop class. It's really good!"

Elizabeth remembered the way Brooke had spoken to Bruce Patman in the cafeteria. "And I'm sure Bruce will want to help, too. Let's call them first thing in the morning."

The girls gossiped and planned most of the night, but were bursting with energy the next day. After a huge breakfast of strawberry pancakes, they raced back to the rec-room. Lila called Jerry and explained their scheme. Everyone crowded around the phone, trying to hear the conversation.

But there wasn't any need to guess how Jerry felt about Jessica's plan. Every girl in the room could hear the loud laughter that came from the receiver as soon as Lila had finished. In fact, Lila told them when she'd hung up, Jerry wanted to start work right away. He was going to phone Bruce and arrange to use his workshop. The two boys would check in with Jessica later that afternoon.

"Meanwhile," Lila informed them, "someone has to go to school and sneak out one of the folding chairs from the gym."

Tamara volunteered. "My brother has a special Boy Scout meeting there this afternoon."

"Perfect!" exclaimed Jessica, eager for an adventure. "I'll go with you, and we'll smuggle the chair over to Bruce's house."

Even though several other girls wanted to share in the fun of this secret mission, they agreed that too many "thieves" would attract attention and double the risk of being caught smuggling the gym chair out of the school. So, it was just Jessica and Tamara who went to the Patman mansion that afternoon. The metal folding chair rested between them as they pressed the bell outside the huge estate on the hill overlooking Sweet Valley.

"Hi, girls." Bruce was wearing jeans and a surfing tee shirt. "Come on down to the workshop. Jerry's already figured out how to make the chair collapse."

Jessica, Tamara, and Bruce hurried out of the marble foyer and down to Mr. Patman's workshop. There, surrounded by drills and craft saws and dozens of other tools, was Jerry. He had sawed a piece of plywood in half, and Jessica and Tamara noticed that there were hinges along the sides of both halves.

"Hey, that's great," said Jessica. "Now, let's see if it works."

After Jerry cut the plywood to fit the chair, he gave the bottom of the chair a few sharp taps with a hammer, and all four tugged and pulled and finally succeeded in removing its seat. Then, ripping the beige vinyl covering from the seat and wrapping it around the hinged plywood, Jerry carefully inserted the new bottom into the chair and stood it upright. "There," he said, looking proud. "Who wants to try it out?"

"Not me," insisted Jessica. "I've taken enough falls to last me for the rest of my life."

"Not me either," said Bruce. "I've supplied the tools. I'm not giving my body to this project, too!"

Jessica and Bruce turned to Tamara. A look of panic crossed her face. "No way," she declared.

"Well," Jerry announced gallantly, "since it's my creation, I'd better be the guinea pig."

Jerry gingerly lowered himself onto the chair. For several seconds the chair supported him. Then, just as he was about to get up and see what had gone wrong, the chair gave way. With a frightening crack, the seat collapsed under him. Jerry looked like a human pretzel. His bottom was on the floor and his feet were sticking up through the empty seat.

"Hooray!" Bruce yelled while the two girls applauded loudly. Jerry smiled and waved.

"It works! It works!" Jessica was thrilled. "I can't wait to see Queen Brooke take a seat on *that* throne!"

"Well," agreed Jerry, picking himself up from the floor, "it's the least we can do for Brooke after all she's done for us. But how are we going to sneak this chair back into the gym?"

"Leave that to me," Jessica assured him. "I'll think of something."

Jessica and the others spent most of that night on the phone. The Sweet Valley grapevine spread the word quickly. Soon everyone knew that the fun was scheduled for the book fair assembly the next day. In fact Jessica spent so much time on the phone that it was quite late before she remembered the problem of the chair. She was on the second sentence of her overdue book report when she got an inspiration and hurried downstairs to the garage.

A few moments later, she poked her head into her twin's bedroom. "Busy, Lizzie?" she asked.

"No, Jess." Elizabeth was bent over her homework. "I'm just doing this history assignment for fun."

"Funny. Very funny, Liz. But I know some- thing even funnier." She turned back toward her own room. "Of course, if you don't want to hear about it . . ."

Elizabeth closed her book. "If I don't want to hear about it," she said with a laugh, "you'll tell me anyway. So let's get on with it. What plot has my brilliant baby sister hatched now?"

"Just a way to have Brooke carry her very own booby-trapped chair to school, that's all." Jessica sank onto her sister's bed, looking very proud of herself.

"What? She'd never agree to drag that chair to school."

"Maybe not a chair, but what if we disguised it as her pal Jennifer's book fair project?"

Elizabeth studied Jessica, who lay with her feet dangling lazily over the sides of the bed. She bent over to look her twin in the eyes. "That's fine with me, as long as *you* play Jennifer."

Jessica lifted her head. Her smile was so broad that the dimple in her left cheek showed. "But, Liz, I have a special Unicorn meeting first thing in the morning. Besides, you're so much better at being friendly to creeps than I am."

"But I've already promised to play Jennifer at the fair, Jess. Why do I have to walk Brooke to school? It's your turn to do that."

"I know, Liz. But I *have* to be at that meeting tomorrow. My whole future depends on it. We're trying to decide on a fund raiser. What happens if

I'm not there and they decide to sell magazine subscriptions? I'd die!"

"I don't care if you end up selling hot dogs, Jess. I'm tired of being somebody's phony best friend. I'm tired of worrying about being caught. And I'll be glad when we've settled things with Brooke, and we can go back to being ourselves."

"We won't have to wait long," promised Jessica. She got off Elizabeth's bed and pulled her twin toward her own room. "And I just found the perfect disguise for the chair." As they stepped through her door, she pointed to a long cardboard carton on the floor. "Remember when Steven made the JV basketball team and begged Mom and Dad for a new backboard to practice on? Well, I found the box it came in behind the rakes in the garage."

Elizabeth had to admit the plan seemed perfect. After all, Jennifer, like all the other kids at school, would have to submit a fair project that morning. The chair would just fit in the box, and the school custodian would surely let the girls drop it off in the gym. Someone could easily sneak back later and set the chair up with the others.

"If you do me this one favor, Liz, I'll never ever ask you for another thing for the rest of my life." Jessica, dancing with excitement, tugged on her sister and handed her the big carton. "I'll even play Jennifer on the phone right now. I'll ask Brooke how the screening was and tell her I need her help tomorrow. I can be as nice as can be when I don't have to face Brooke in person."

While Elizabeth packed the folding chair in the carton, Jessica called Brooke. In a voice as sweet as honey, she told Brooke that she'd finished a really special project for the fair and that her sisters were both busy the next morning.

A few minutes later Jessica hung up. Her expression didn't match the gentle voice she had used on the phone. "Of all the nerve!" she exclaimed. "Would you believe what that gross girl just said?"

Elizabeth, who had scrawled "book fair" in big letters across the face of the carton, stood up to examine her work. "What's the matter?" she asked when she saw the furious scowl Jessica wore.

"Brooke. That's what's the matter! She just told me she'd be glad to help!"

"So? That's great."

"But you didn't hear *why* she wants to help." Jessica was so angry she crumpled up the piece of notepaper she'd started her book report on. "She said she hopes my project is good enough to win the book fair award, so everyone in school will forget about that spoiled crybaby Jessica!"

The next day all Brooke talked about on the way to school was the accident to the poster and how Jessica had ruined Brooke's chances to make friends at the new school. "As soon as your crybaby sister got through with them, every kid in that room thought I'd ruined her dumb poster on purpose." Brooke walked behind Elizabeth, who held the front of the heavy box. She wore a red bow behind her ear to match the oversize cardigan she'd borrowed from Steven.

"Maybe, if you'd just apologized right away," Elizabeth suggested, "the whole thing would have been forgotten by now."

"Are you kidding?" Brooke laughed bitterly. "Do you think Jessica would give up a chance for all those sympathy votes? No way! She's just using me to get more attention." She paused and raised her end of the box as they came to a curb. "As if she needed any more!"

Elizabeth kept quiet. She knew that if she said anything, it would probably give her away. She wanted to tell Brooke off, to make her understand that she had no right to judge someone so harshly and unfairly. Instead, she remained silent, just nodding her head as Brooke kept ranting. Once, though, when Brooke called Jessica a "two-faced phony," Elizabeth got so mad she dropped the front end of the box with a thud.

As the box hit the ground, the chair inside landed with a metallic thud. "What on earth have you got in here?" asked Brooke. "It sure doesn't feel like a poster. What did you do, Jennifer, build a printing press?"

Elizabeth was so angry she couldn't think of a good answer. "It—it's a surprise," she told Brooke. "Just wait until the book fair assembly after lunch. I think you'll really like it."

"Well," Brooke admitted as they arrived at the school and headed for the gymnasium door, "I don't even have to like it. Just as long as it wins." They handed the box to the custodian and then circled around to the front entrance to wait for the first bell. "After all, if another Wakefield wins the prize, maybe Jessica will stop hogging the spotlight."

Elizabeth nearly exploded. "What do you care?" She couldn't believe Brooke was so jealous of the attention Jessica was getting when she herself never made any effort to make people like her at all. "It doesn't matter to you what anyone here thinks, anyway."

"It matters what *you* think, Jennifer," Brooke told her as the bell rang and they started up the front steps. "I'd feel sort of proud to watch you win that prize. See you later." She waved and walked off down the hall. Elizabeth waved back, wondering why Brooke always made her feel sad and angry at the same time.

Eight

◇

After math class, Jessica and Lila met Elizabeth in the hallway. They were both giggling and breathless. "It's time to set up Queen Brooke's throne," Jessica announced.

"Everything's set for her majesty's coronation." Lila was bubbling with the excitement of their plot. "I've told everyone about it."

Jessica held up a roll of black tape she'd brought with her. "We'll just stick a piece of this to the back of the chair, Liz, and you'll have no trouble spotting it when we come in for the assembly."

As the three sixth graders started off toward the gym, Elizabeth wasn't so sure her role as Jennifer was to her liking. "I don't know," she told the others. "It may not be so easy."

"What do you mean?" Jessica stopped walking and stared at her sister. "Everything's just right."

"Maybe," admitted her twin. "But it seems like kind of a dirty trick. Do you know Brooke told me on the way to school that she wished the accident with your poster had never happened."

Lila was outraged. "After all she's said and done, I'd say we've been pretty patient. And I, for one, am tired of waiting. I'm ready to see her get what she deserves—*now!*"

"Liz," Jessica explained, "we all know what a softie you are. And you know that if Mr. Bowman hadn't picked me to present the poster award, I'd be glad to play Jennifer and polish off that monster all by myself." She looked fondly at her twin, and then at Lila. "But I guess I'm going to have to settle for standing right up front while my own terrific sister gives Brooke what she deserves."

Elizabeth wanted to please her twin. But somehow she couldn't think of Brooke as so bad anymore. "It just doesn't seem fair, though. So many of us, all picking on Brooke."

"Hey," corrected Lila, "I think you've got it backwards, Elizabeth. It's Brooke who's been doing the picking, and she's pretty nearly managed to be nasty to every single kid in the sixth grade."

Jessica looped her arm through Elizabeth's and guided her into the darkened gym while Lila turned on the lights and began to look for the carton containing the chair. "You wouldn't let your own little sister down, would you, Liz?"

Elizabeth knew what her father would say. She still recalled his words at their dinner that weekend: "You can't always tell why people are

nasty. Brooke may not be as tough as she seems."
But her father hadn't heard Brooke yell at Bruce,
she told herself. He hadn't watched her hurt Lila
and just about everyone else. Most of all, he
hadn't seen that smile on Brooke's face when Jessica had fallen in the gym. "No," she told her twin
now, as they unfolded the chair and set it up in the
front row, "I won't let you down, Jess."

After Jessica had fixed the tape to the chair,
the three left the gym and Elizabeth raced to her
first class. Just outside the door, she felt a tap on
her shoulder and turned to find Brooke beside her.

"Excuse me, Elizabeth," Brooke told her. "I've
been looking for Jennifer everywhere. Have you
seen her?"

Elizabeth knew the red cardigan and bow
were safely stowed in her locker. "No, I haven't,"
she said in her own voice, glad not to have to
whisper as Jennifer always did.

Brooke looked pale and a little worried. "Well,
if you see her, will you ask her to meet me for
lunch?" Again, a tiny, worried frown crossed her
face. "It's kind of important."

Elizabeth promised she'd tell Jennifer. All
through the period Elizabeth debated with herself.
Should she get the sweater and bow out of her
locker and meet Brooke for lunch? Or would it be
better just to pretend that Elizabeth never found
Jennifer at all? She didn't feel like playing Jennifer
anymore. She was feeling so relieved that the assembly would be the Wakefield triplets' farewell
performance.

But Brooke found her as soon as the lunch bell
rang. "Don't forget," she told her. "I really need to

see Jennifer." Something urgent in her tone made Elizabeth decide to meet her after all.

She found Brooke by herself at a table near the door to the cafeteria, with nothing but a drink and two silver foil packages on her lunch tray. "Why aren't you eating?" Elizabeth asked in Jennifer's soft voice.

"I guess I don't really feel like it," Brooke told her. "Come on, Jennifer, let's go outside. I've got something you can eat in here." She picked up the foil packages, and Elizabeth followed her out to the hilly lawn behind the school.

It was pleasant, Elizabeth had to admit, to lie back in the grass and stare at the old brick building against the blue sky.

"I come here a lot," Brooke said, waving her hand at the secluded nook behind the gardening shed. "It's a good place for thinking."

Elizabeth thought of her "thinking seat" in the old pine tree in the Wakefields' backyard. She knew what it was like to have a special place to come to. She also knew that people usually came to this kind of place when something was wrong.

"What's on your mind, Brooke? You look pretty down today."

"Oh, nothing really," Brooke told her, unwrapping one of the foil packages and handing the other to Elizabeth. "It's just the birthday blues, I guess."

Elizabeth stared at the foil on Brooke's lap. It held a huge slice of chocolate cake, covered with white icing and decorated with blue flowers. "That's right," she said, pretending to sound surprised, "today's your birthday." Slowly, she opened her own package and found another piece of cake. Feeling suddenly very embarrassed, she smiled awkwardly at Brooke. "Gee, what a pretty cake. I love chocolate."

"I hate it, but Dad didn't even ask me what kind I wanted. He just phoned in an order to the best bakery in town and had them deliver it this morning." Brooke's eyes closed, and Elizabeth thought she saw tears brimming at their edges.

"I'm sorry I forgot your birthday, Brooke. But your family remembered and that's what counts."

Brooke looked at Elizabeth. "What family?" she asked. "The bakery's delivery man was the only one who wished me a happy birthday today." Her voice caught as if she were trying not to cry. "Not that I care," she said, clearly fighting tears, "but my dad wasn't even home this morning. He had another script conference in Hollywood. I wish we'd never moved."

"It's hard when you've got busy, working parents," Elizabeth agreed.

"At least you've got two parents who care." Brooke's expression was angry now, despite the tears in her eyes. "My mother doesn't care about me at all. In fact, she wants to hurt me as much as she can."

Elizabeth didn't know anything about Mrs. Dennis. In all their conversations Brooke had never mentioned her mother. Elizabeth had assumed she was dead. "What do you mean, Brooke? I'm sure your mother doesn't want to hurt you."

Brooke was crying openly now, tears coursing down her pretty face. "Then why did she leave me? She said she'd come see me as soon as she could, but why did she ever agree to leave?"

Elizabeth thought of all the mean things Brooke had said to the kids in school. She understood all the hate and anger that was packed inside the new girl. Now, for the first time, what her father had told them began to make sense. Maybe Brooke didn't have as much as she seemed to. Maybe she had less than anyone.

"My parents got divorced a few years ago. When my mom remarried, the judge told her I couldn't move to Europe with her. He said that dad got custody of me in the divorce and he would have to agree to my going away." As she spoke, Brooke looked softer and more vulnerable than Elizabeth had ever seen her. "Mom was going to have a baby, and she chose to go with her husband and leave me behind. She didn't call me today. She didn't even send a card."

Brooke rolled over onto her stomach and put her head in her hands. Elizabeth had the strangest urge to reach over and pat her head. Brooke seemed so small and unhappy, lying there. But then Elizabeth remembered how badly Brooke had treated Jessica. She wished she had never agreed to have lunch with Brooke.

Suddenly Brooke raised her head and looked steadily at Elizabeth. "Do you know what, Jennifer?" she asked, her voice trembling. "You're the first friend I've ever had."

And Jennifer doesn't exist at all, Elizabeth thought miserably.

"At least since grade school," Brooke continued. "After my mom left, I sort of figured nobody would like me anymore, since I could never get my mom to do the same kind of stuff moms usually do." She tore a fistful of grass from the lawn and flung it defiantly toward the school. "And if nobody's going to like me, I'm sure not going to like them. Especially Jessica. Everybody loves her. She's got everything, and I've got nothing. I just hate being me!" Now she buried her head again and sobbed into the grass.

Elizabeth's father had been right after all. Brooke Dennis wasn't as lucky as everyone thought. They had all made a terrible mistake, and it was up to Elizabeth to correct it. "I'm so sorry," she told Brooke, and she meant it.

"I'm just glad I have someone I can at least talk to." Brooke sat up and dried her eyes with the back of one fingernail-polished hand. "You must think I'm an awful baby, Jennifer. But every time we move it starts all over. I just know everyone will hate me, and they always do. I have to act tough and pretend I don't care, but sometimes, like now, it's really rough."

"I'll bet if you weren't so sure people were going to dislike you," Elizabeth suggested gently, "they might get a chance to know you better."

"I don't think so. That first day when I saw Jessica coming down the street with that dumpy little dog, I knew what Sweet Valley was going to be like. My mom raises show dogs, and she must care more about them than me, because she's still got her dogs but she doesn't have me."

"But you didn't give Jess a chance."

"I didn't need to," Brooke insisted. "I took one look at Jessica, and I knew she had a mother who didn't care about silly, skinny show dogs. That fat old dog just made me want to cry right on the spot. And when Jessica said hello in that super-friendly way, I figured she was trying to make me like her just so she could be nasty later."

Elizabeth knew she had a lot of explaining to do. But she knew she had something more important to do first. Somehow she had to stop their trick during the assembly. If Brooke's new best friend tricked her she'd never trust anyone again. The chip on Brooke's shoulder had to be knocked off with kindness and understanding, not a cruel joke.

Now Brooke was standing and brushing the cake crumbs and grass from her crisply pleated skirt. "I feel better, Jennifer. I sure wish you could have been in some of my classes. I miss having you to talk to."

Elizabeth felt more guilty and horrible than she could ever remember feeling. She wanted to sink into the ground, but more than that she wanted to make things better for Brooke Dennis. "Come on," she said, pulling Brooke by the hand. "Let's skip the assembly and have a nice, long talk at my house. No one will miss us."

But Brooke stood still and pulled away from Elizabeth. "No way, Jennifer. You worked hard on that big project we lugged to school this morning. And I'll bet you stand a good chance of winning the award." She smiled the first genuine smile Elizabeth had seen on her face since they'd met.

Jessica's plan, Elizabeth realized, had worked too well. Since she had helped carry Jennifer's project, Brooke was determined to see it win. Unwillingly, she felt herself being dragged along by an enthusiastic Brooke. "I hate crowds," Elizabeth said, desperately trying to keep Brooke from heading for the gym. "What if I win and make a fool of myself in front of all those people?"

"Don't worry," Brooke assured her, linking her arm through Elizabeth's as they walked in through the gym door. "If you feel a little scared when you get up to accept the award, just look back at the audience. You'll have a friend right up in the front row, cheering for you!"

Nine

◇

Elizabeth looked around the gym. The bleachers had been folded back, and chairs were set up around the stage. Mr. Bowman, the principal, and Jessica were seated near a microphone onstage, where the presentation would take place. As the two girls walked through the crowd, familiar faces turned to greet Jennifer and her friend.

"Hey, Jennifer, how's it going?" Charlie Cashman winked at Elizabeth and pointed to the front row of chairs. "If you hurry you can get the last two seats left in the house."

Elizabeth smiled nervously and tried to steer Brooke to an empty seat she spotted in the last row. She had decided that she couldn't let Brooke sit in the chair Jerry had prepared. Not now that Elizabeth understood how unhappy and confused her new neighbor was. Brooke trusted her and needed her friendship. Elizabeth wouldn't let her down.

"Here, Brooke," she said. "Let's sit back here. I hate being right up front."

"Don't be silly, Jen." Brooke laughed and showed Elizabeth the same sweet smile she'd worn a few minutes before. "There's only *one* chair here. Besides, you'll need to be right up front if you win the award."

"All right, then. I'll go up front, but I'll die if I see you watching me." Elizabeth knew she sounded ridiculous, but she was determined to save Brooke from the trap that had been set for her. "Please, Brooke, sit here. I'll meet you right after the assembly."

As the girls stood in the aisle beside the empty chair, a boy ran toward them from several rows up. It was Bruce Patman. He was moving at top speed as if he were headed for the finish line in a race. "Excuse me, ladies," he said, panting. "This seat is taken."

Elizabeth ignored Bruce's broad smile and insisted that the seat was empty. "I saw you sitting next to Jerry McAllister," she told him.

"Yeah," added Brooke, putting on her tough act as soon as she saw Bruce. "You may think you're the greatest thing on earth, but even *you* can't sit in two chairs at once."

"He doesn't need to," said a voice from behind them. "He was saving that seat for *me*." Lila Fowler swept past them and plopped down on the vacant chair. Elizabeth's heart sank as she watched Lila fold her skirt daintily over her crossed legs and turn to Brooke. "I'm sure you'll enjoy the ceremony much more from the front of the room, Brooke. After all, we couldn't let someone like you travel anything but first class."

Now the only two chairs left were the two front-row seats. Brooke angrily headed for the front of the room, and Elizabeth made a desperate decision. Just as her friend was about to sink into the seat with the black tape on its back, Elizabeth grabbed her arm.

"I want that seat, Brooke." Expecting an argument, she pulled Brooke away from the rigged chair and stood in front of it. But, surprisingly, Brooke agreed.

"OK, Jennifer. I don't care which seat I have. If you want that chair, you can have it." As Mr. Bowman started to call for quiet, Brooke sat down in the other chair.

But Jessica was not about to be cheated out of watching Brooke get punished. Springing from her place on the stage, Jessica raced down the steps and right to the two girls. She grabbed Elizabeth's arm and tugged her away from the booby-trapped chair.

"No, Liz, you can't sit there," her twin whispered. "It'll ruin everything."

Quickly, Jessica told Brooke the one thing that she knew would make her get in the booby-trapped chair. "I'm sorry," she said in a loud, firm tone. "Neither of you can sit in that chair." She put her hand over the seat of the chair, knowing Brooke would then insist on sitting there. "It's reserved."

As Jessica scrambled back beside Mr. Bowman, Brooke pushed Elizabeth into the safe chair and sat on the chair Jerry and Bruce had made. "This is still a public school," she scolded, all the resentment back in her face and voice. "No one can push you and me around, Jennifer."

Elizabeth held her breath, too unhappy to move. Maybe, she thought, as Mr. Bowman started to speak, everything would work out. Maybe Jerry's trap wouldn't work.

"And, now, I'm going to ask someone who worked very hard on a poster of her own to present this special award." Mr. Bowman smiled out at the sea of faces in the gym and then held out his arm to Jessica. "Jessica Wakefield, if you'll do the honors."

He handed Jessica the envelope with the book club membership and gift certificate enclosed. "The winner's name is right on the envelope. If you'll just read it aloud to the group."

The whole school watched as Jessica took the envelope and read its cover. Jessica's expression changed from somber to overjoyed. "It says Jessica Wakefield," she said. "There must be some mistake. I—"

"No mistake at all, Jessica," Mr. Bowman assured her. "The judging committee all agreed that your project, until it was destroyed, showed the most work, neatness, and originality of all those submitted." He faced Jessica and applauded.

The students in the gym joined him, and Jessica smiled and blushed. Elizabeth forgot all about Brooke in her excitement. It was wonderful! Jessica's hard work hadn't been for nothing. She felt as happy as if she had won the prize herself. Standing in her seat, she clapped loudly, beaming at her twin.

She remembered Brooke when she noticed her new friend was on her feet, too. Clapping with everyone else, Brooke exchanged happy grins with Elizabeth. "Maybe now Jessica won't be so mad at me," she said. "I'm really glad, Jen." As the applause subsided and Mr. Bowman stepped once more to the mike, Brooke sat back down.

With a sickening crack, the false bottom of the rigged chair collapsed, and Brooke fell through her seat. She sat on the floor in the hushed gym, with her feet sticking foolishly out of the empty chair bottom. The silence was replaced by titters and then chuckles and finally loud laughter. Brooke looked over at her friend. Suddenly, all the foolish arguments over the chair made sense. "You knew about this!" The pain and hurt that showed on Brooke's face made Elizabeth wish she were anywhere else in the world.

As the classmates she had snubbed continued to have the last laugh, Brooke tried to lift herself from the shattered chair. Elizabeth, dizzy with guilt, leaned over to help her up. "Don't touch me!" screamed the humiliated girl. "I don't need your help. I don't need anybody's help at all!"

Suddenly Mr. Bowman was by her side. "Here, Brooke, let's see if we can straighten you out." Trying to joke her out of her embarrassment and smiling kindly, he offered Brooke his hand. "Looks like you had a little trouble with your chair."

"It wasn't an accident," explained Brooke,

who was crying openly. "It was Jennifer." Her old anger was back. "*She* did this to me. It's all her fault." She pointed at Elizabeth.

"You mean Elizabeth made your chair break?" Mr. Bowman put his arm around Brooke, who had now begun to sob. "I don't think anyone's to blame, Brooke."

"*She* is," whimpered Brooke. "Jennifer knew about it all along."

"This is Elizabeth," Mr. Bowman corrected her, and smiled. "This time I'm sure because her twin is still up on stage."

"It's Jennifer," insisted Brooke, not realizing how badly she'd been tricked. "They're not twins. They're triplets."

The students in the seats nearby couldn't contain themselves. They roared with laughter at Brooke's confusion.

"Well, I admit that sometimes it may seem like there are three Wakefields in this school," conceded Mr. Bowman. "But I'm afraid Jessica and Elizabeth are the only Wakefields here."

At first, Brooke seemed to refuse to believe she'd been tricked. "No," she said, shaking her head. "This is Jennifer." Then, looking at Elizabeth's sorrowful, guilty expression and hearing the howls of laughter that surrounded her, Brooke finally realized the truth.

"How could you?" she asked, whirling to face the laughing students around her. "How could you?" At last she turned back to Elizabeth, who stood with her head bent, too ashamed to look Brooke in the face.

Then Brooke was gone, racing like a whirlwind down the aisle and out the gym door. It happened so quickly that hardly anyone noticed her go.

Elizabeth knew how very wrong they'd been about Brooke. She had been the one person who might have stopped them, but she had failed. Now she wondered how she could explain this terrible joke to Brooke. And whether Brooke could ever forgive her.

Elizabeth raced after Brooke. She had to stop her and make her understand.

But it was no use. As soon as she caught up to her neighbor, she saw the old stubborn expression on Brooke's face.

"Please, Brooke," Elizabeth begged. "Let me explain."

"Listen Jennifer or Elizabeth or Jessica or whoever you are," she screamed, "I don't want any explanations. Just get away and leave me alone." She turned on her heel and took off across the lawn.

Dismayed, Elizabeth watched Brooke disappear from sight. She stood by herself for a while, wondering why she had ever agreed to do such an awful thing. What had she thought a dumb stunt like that would accomplish anyway?

Elizabeth looked for Brooke for the next fifteen minutes. Then Elizabeth thought of her own "thinking seat" and remembered Brooke's secret spot behind the gardening shed. Sure enough, Elizabeth found the girl sitting with her head in her hands in the same place where they had had lunch together. She was sobbing uncontrollably and didn't even look up when Elizabeth sat down beside her. This time, Elizabeth didn't resist the urge to comfort the girl. She put her arm around Brooke and let her cry on her shoulder.

At last Brooke looked up at Elizabeth, two long tear stains trailing down her cheeks. "I thought you were my friend," she said quietly. "How could you let them do that to me? How could you lie to me like that?"

"I tried to stop them today, Brooke. Honest. Once I knew what you were really like, I didn't want to go through with it. It's just that things had gone too far."

"You bet they did. I just want to disappear." Brooke sniffed and wiped her tear-streaked face. "I want to go somewhere where no one can ever hurt me again—not my mother, not my father, not you, or anyone at all."

"I'm so sorry," Elizabeth said, feeling worse than she could ever imagine feeling. "I'd like us to still be friends, Brooke," she said sincerely. "Can't we start over?"

"What's the use? I'd have to go through this all again. Nothing's different. Everybody still hates me."

"I don't," Elizabeth told her.

"Who are you, anyway?"

"I'm Elizabeth, and I'd like to be your friend if you'd let me. I know it seems hard to believe, but I really do care what happens to you."

"Well, you're the only one. Even I don't care anymore." Brooke struggled to her feet and walked off without looking back.

Ten

◇

When Elizabeth got home, her mother and sister were waiting for her. The look on Mrs. Wakefield's face made it plain that something was terribly wrong. Jessica was seated at the kitchen table, a glum expression on her face. There was no after-school snack or homework spread across the table. Instead, mother and daughter sat stiffly in their chairs, their hands folded in front of them. Clearly, a family conference was about to be called.

"Mr. Dennis has just phoned me with some very bad news," Mrs. Wakefield began. "I'm hoping you and Jessica can make it better."

Jessica looked helplessly at her twin. Elizabeth, too depressed to be upset, sank heavily into the empty chair by her mother.

"I thought that you two had outgrown foolish

look-alike games. Especially ones that hurt others," Mrs. Wakefield said in a gentle, sad voice that always made the girls feel much guiltier than if she yelled and scolded. "Brooke's father tells me she's been the victim of a cruel joke. And it seems you girls were behind it. I hope Mr. Dennis is mistaken."

Jessica hung her head, but Elizabeth looked straight at her mother. "He's not, Mom. I don't think Brooke will ever trust anyone again, and it's all our fault."

Steven burst through the door and opened the refrigerator as the twins were reviewing the whole story for their mother. Then Elizabeth described what she had learned about Brooke's family problems. At last, everyone began to understand why their new neighbor had been so unpleasant.

"Well," Mrs. Wakefield began, "it sounds as if Brooke's a very confused young lady. I, for one, intend to have a long talk with that busy father of hers." Mrs. Wakefield studied her two fair-haired daughters. "How about you? If I know you two, you won't let Brooke stay hurting for long."

Jessica looked perplexed. "But what can we do, Mom? Brooke is so mad at both of us, she'll never speak to either of us again."

"That's right," Elizabeth agreed. "And the horrible part is, I don't blame her one bit."

"Maybe she'd still speak to Jennifer," Steven suggested, his face brightening.

Now it was Mrs. Wakefield's turn to be puzzled. "What do you mean, Steve? It was that made-up triplet who started all the trouble in the first place."

"That's just why she should be the one to finish it."

"But we both played Jennifer," explained Elizabeth. "How could two Jennifers apologize to Brooke?"

"Easy," their brother told her. "You both dress up as Jennifer and make her understand you're double sorry. Show her she's got two real friends now instead of one phony one."

"How about lots of real friends?" asked Jessica, now enthusiastic. "I'll bet a lot of kids at school will want to make it up to Brooke, too."

Elizabeth brightened. Even if Brooke wouldn't listen to the two of them, she'd have to believe they were serious if the others joined them. "You're right, Jess. I think this calls for an emergency first meeting of the Brooke Dennis fan club."

"Now you're cooking, big sister. How many kids do you think we could get over here to help?"

Elizabeth grinned broadly. "If we tell Caroline Pearce, we could probably have the whole school here in no time!"

A few short hours later, the Wakefields' living room was filled with kids from school. After Elizabeth told them how lonely Brooke was, they all felt awful about having ganged up on her. "Especially on her birthday," moaned Julie Porter. "What a day to make someone cry!"

"Looks like we really goofed," admitted Jerry

McAllister. "I wish I hadn't done such a good job on that chair," he added. "I feel terrible."

"We've got an idea!" Caroline Pearce linked arms with Amy and Elizabeth, then called for silence. "We've thought of how to show Brooke we're sorry."

Everyone gathered around the three girls, and Steven and Mrs. Wakefield, who had just carried in a fresh supply of popcorn, stayed to hear the new plan. "It's simple," Caroline told them all. "We'll give Brooke another birthday surprise, only this time it will be the right kind. We'll throw her the biggest, best birthday party ever."

"Sounds good," commented Steven. "But just how do you expect to get Brooke over here? I mean, she's not exactly on speaking terms with anybody here."

"Don't worry about that," Mrs. Wakefield promised. "I can speak to Mr. Dennis and make certain he brings Brooke here. How does that sound?"

"Great!" exclaimed Amy. "I love birthday parties!"

"Well, this one's going to be a little short on food, unless I get to the store." Mrs. Wakefield smiled at the sea of eager faces around her. "Any orders?"

"How about tacos?"

"Potato chips!"

"Wait a minute." Mrs. Wakefield laughed and picked up a pad and pencil from the coffee table. "Let's write everything down."

Mary Giaccio raced to her side, taking the tab-

let from her hand. "That's OK, Mrs. Wakefield,"
she volunteered. "I'll do this for you and then
we'll both go to the store. I love shopping."

"And while we're at it, what about the cake?"
Mrs. Wakefield asked.

"That's where *we* come in," Elizabeth told her.
She looked at Amy and Julie, who nodded their
approval, and continued. "If this is going to be a
surprise party, we'd like the cake to be the best
surprise of all."

Mrs. Wakefield beamed with pride at her
daughters and their friends. They had made a big
mistake, but they were making up for it in a big
way. She hugged Jessica, who gave a little embarrassed laugh and pushed her mother and Mary
toward the door. "OK, Mom, you two have tons of
shopping to do. The rest of us have some serious
baking ahead of us."

"That's right," Elizabeth agreed. "If we're going to have a vanilla cake with orange frosting by
tonight, we'd better get to it."

"Hey, why not chocolate?" complained
Steven.

"I'm afraid it'll have to be vanilla tonight,"
Elizabeth told him, as she led the group into the
Wakefields' Spanish-tiled kitchen. "I know for a
fact that Brooke hates chocolate.

"Oh, yeah?" Steven sounded disappointed.
"And just who told you that?"

Elizabeth smiled at her brother. "Brooke's first
real friend, that's who."

The whole crew noisily and busily worked at
their various jobs. Finally, Caroline Pearce stood

back to admire their efforts. Everyone agreed that this was going to be the best birthday party ever!

Amy and Caroline had hung yellow-and-pink crepe paper from one end of the living room to the other. Lila had wanted to include the Unicorn color, purple, in their decorating scheme, but several other girls had talked her out of it. Bowls of popcorn and candy topped every table. Balloons hung in a huge cluster from the ceiling.

Below the star, in the middle of the room, was the main attraction. A huge cake, covered with tiny roses and white candles, sat atop a draped stand. Elizabeth's kitchen brigade had outdone themselves. Steven couldn't resist sampling the icing and the broad smile on his face told them the cake tasted as good as it looked.

When Mary and Mrs. Wakefield returned from the store, they could hardly believe their eyes. "You've really outdone yourselves," the twins' mother told them. "Isn't this great?" she asked, turning to Mary.

Mary grinned and held Mrs. Wakefield's arm. "Those decorations sure look nice!" Her eyes were glued on Mrs. Wakefield's friendly face. "I think we should finish unloading the groceries. And then I can help you put everything out." She pulled Mrs. Wakefield by the hand, leading her toward the kitchen.

Jessica nudged Elizabeth. "Boy, I didn't know Mary was such a mother's helper."

Elizabeth studied the blond girl hurrying into the kitchen with her mother. "Neither did I. I can't imagine wanting to help unload groceries!"

"Yeah. Who'd rather spend time helping a grown-up than being in here, where the action is?"

"Right now, me!" Elizabeth dashed into the hall and opened the front door for her father. She took his briefcase and led him into the living room, where he looked around in confusion. He surveyed the balloons and streamers and then winked at his young guests. "Really, you shouldn't have gone to all this trouble," he joked. "I didn't even win my case today."

Jessica hugged her father, then joined in the fun. "Daddy," she told him, "you don't need to win a case to have a celebration. We're just glad you're home."

"Right, Dad," Steven added, laying an affectionate hand on his father's shoulder, "this was no trouble at all. In fact, a raise in allowance would be enough reward."

Everyone laughed, ready for fun after their hard work. But Mrs. Wakefield had bad news for them. "I'm sorry, kids," she announced, coming back from the kitchen. "But it seems that the birthday girl is in no mood for a party."

"What?" The group was suddenly silent as they all stared at one another in disbelief. Could all their work have been for nothing?

"I just got off the phone with Mr. Dennis. He says he's tried to convince Brooke to join us for a decorating conference tonight. But she won't set foot in this house."

"But, Mom," Jessica cried, "she's just got to come!"

"I guess you've played one trick too many, after all." Mrs. Wakefield sighed. "Brooke told her father she doesn't ever want to see you or Elizabeth again for as long as she lives."

Eleven

◇

As everyone stood in the Wakefields' living room looking helpless, Elizabeth took charge. "Well," she decided, "if Brooke won't come to us, we'll have to go to her." Quickly, she raced upstairs. A minute later she raced downstairs again, grabbed Jessica by the arm, and hustled her into the hall. "Come on, little sister, we've got work to do." From the front door she turned back to the others. "Don't anybody go away. We'll be right back with the guest of honor."

"I hope you know what you're doing," Jessica complained as they hurried down their driveway and up the street. "Hey, that's not the way to Brooke's house." She stopped in the middle of the sidewalk as her sister headed off in the wrong direction.

"I know," Elizabeth told her. "But it is the way to Mrs. Bramble's."

Mrs. Bramble was the elderly woman whose cocker spaniel was the dog Jessica had been walking the day she first met Brooke. The lively old woman had become a special friend of the twins', but Jessica didn't see how she could help them now.

"If we're going to convince Brooke to even speak to us," explained Elizabeth, "we're going to need to make an extra-special impression. That's why I brought these along." She pulled three bright red bows from her pocket. Jessica stared at the shiny ribbons, each exactly like the ones Jennifer had worn.

"If Brooke hates *two* Jennifers," she asked, "what makes you think she'll like *three*? And what makes you think Mrs. Bramble is going to wear one of those silly bows?"

"She's not going to, Jess. Sally is."

Sally was Mrs. Bramble's aged dog, and Jessica was more confused than ever. Still, she tagged along as Elizabeth rang Mrs. Bramble's bell and asked to "borrow" Sally. Soon the three of them were on their way to Brooke's house. They made quite a picture, two blond identical twins and a fat, shaggy old dog— all with red bows behind their ears!

It was such a ridiculous picture that even Brooke couldn't help smiling a tiny bit when she opened the door. But the smile was replaced by a scowl. "If you think I'm going to ask you in so you can make a fool of me again," she told them defiantly, "you are dead wrong."

"That's OK, Brooke," Elizabeth told her. "I don't think I'd let us in if I were you, either." She made Sally sit and held tight to her leash to make sure she didn't wander. "Jessica and Sally and I just came by to try to show you how sorry we are. We'll be glad to apologize from out here, if you'll just listen."

Jessica looked over Brooke's shoulder and saw Mr. Dennis peering at them from the hall. He winked kindly at her, and Jessica hoped he would have time to help Brooke now. "Please, Brooke," she said, "we'd really like to start over."

"That's right," urged Elizabeth. "You remember when you first saw Jessica and Sally walking down this street? Remember how it seemed Jessica had everything you didn't, including an old dog who wasn't anything like your mom's show dogs?"

A look of sadness crossed Brooke's face.

"Well, we just want you to know that things aren't always what they seem." Elizabeth leaned down to pet Sally, whose red bow had fallen under her chin and who covered Elizabeth's face with sloppy dog kisses. "Old Sally here isn't our dog." Sally, finished with Elizabeth, moved over to Brooke and began licking her ankles. This time, though, the girl didn't try to kick Sally, but knelt instead to stroke her old, brown head.

"That's right," Jessica told her. "She belongs to a woman who lives on Shady Dale Court. And, Brooke, more important than that, we've decided that our first impressions of you were wrong, too."

Brooke looked up, surprised. "What do you mean, Elizabeth?" she asked.

"I'm not Elizabeth, I'm Jessica. And I mean that I thought you were just about the nastiest, meanest person I'd ever met in my life." She smiled with embarrassment at Brooke. "I mean all your perfect clothes, your famous father, and your beautiful house. You had so much more than I did, but you still couldn't be nice to people."

Brooke looked amazed. "More than you! How could you possibly think that?" She leaned against the door frame, trying to figure everything out. "It's you who has everything—a mother who loves you, a father who's always around. And on top of that, every kid in school thinks you're terrific. What more could you want?"

Mr. Dennis stepped up from behind his daughter and put his arm gently on her shoulder. "I think you kids just had your wires crossed, that's all." Then he shook his head. "And you weren't the only ones. I was so busy trying to make you a good home, Brooke, that I forgot to live in it with you." He tousled Brooke's perfectly combed hair. "I even forgot to tell you how much your mother loves you."

Brooke turned to him, a tiny, hopeful question mark in her eyes. "Why, what do you mean, Dad? Mommy left us."

"Yes, you know she did. But you also know she needed time with her new husband and baby. What you don't know, Brooke, is that she's planning to visit us this summer. She asked me to keep it a secret, so you'd be surprised." He took his daughter's hand and led her friends into the living room. "But I think we've had enough surprises around here lately."

"Well, almost enough." Jessica giggled happily.

"We've got just one more for you, Brooke, if you'll only come back to the house with us." Elizabeth's smile was so genuine that even Brooke couldn't doubt her.

".OK, Jessica," she said. "Just as long as Daddy can come too. And," she added, winking, "if you promise I get a *real* chair to sit in!"

"I'm Elizabeth," Elizabeth corrected her, "and it's a deal."

"How am I ever going to get you two straight?" Brooke asked, smiling from one new friend to the other.

"We're still sorting things out ourselves," admitted Jessica. "This triplet business was triple confusing. It sure is good to be back to twins again!"

Back at the Wakefields' house, Caroline Pearce was peering through the living-room curtains. When the twins, Brooke, and Mr. Dennis came into view, Caroline gave a little shriek and headed for cover. "Quick!" she yelled, "everybody hide!"

When Elizabeth and Jessica invited their guests in, the whole house seemed strangely still. But just as the group entered the living room, everyone leaped from his hiding place. "Surprise!"

Everyone could see how shocked Brooke was as she was suddenly surrounded by her new friends. Flushed and smiling, Brooke turned from one friendly face to another.

"I really don't know what to say," she told them quietly. With a glowing face, she studied the loops of crepe paper and the colorful cluster of balloons hanging over her head. "Oooh." She took a shy step forward toward the cake on its draped platform.

"Don't worry," Charlie assured her. "It won't explode." He made one of his comic bows and then presented her with a knife. "But we will, if you don't hurry up and cut the first piece!"

Everybody laughed and gathered around Brooke and her birthday cake. They sang a chorus of "Happy Birthday" as Brooke stared at the pink roses that had been squeezed into the shape of a heart on the cake. In the center of each rose, glowing brightly, was a birthday candle. "Shouldn't I blow them out?" she asked.

"Sure!" Now her friends stepped back as Brooke took a deep breath and leaned over the cake. She blew out all the candles with one try.

"That means you'll get your wish today!" Jessica announced, starting to pull the candles from the middle of the roses.

"I'll cut the cake for you, Brooke," said Mrs. Wakefield. "I'd hate to see those gorgeous clothes get ruined."

"Thanks," Brooke spoke softly. Then she smiled mischievously. "But if you left me on my own, maybe I would ruin this awful dress and be able to get some comfortable clothes instead!"

Everyone chuckled except Mr. Dennis. "But I thought the clothes Mrs. Dubois picked out were very stylish." He looked confused.

"They are, Daddy," Brooke told him. "That's just the trouble. These clothes are pretty to look at, but they're not much fun to wear!" She hugged her father affectionately and looked happier than anyone in Sweet Valley could ever remember seeing her.

From the back of the room, Steven offered to help. "Until you trade in those designer clothes, Brooke, maybe Jennifer's wardrobe would come in handy." He whirled around like a model, displaying the red cardigan he had lent the twins for their triplets trick. "You can borrow my sweaters anytime."

As the laughter died down, everyone began to eat the slices of cake that Brooke passed around. With everyone in the room served, Brooke settled down to enjoy her own piece. Just as she was about to swallow her first bite, though, a last-minute guest reminded her that she'd forgotten someone.

Yelping and wiggling at her feet, Sally begged for her own cake to help celebrate. Brooke laughed and placed a paper plate heaped with cake beside the little dog. "We wouldn't want to forget you," she told Sally. "If Jessica and Elizabeth can be big enough to apologize, I can too." She leaned down to give the old cocker spaniel a tickle under its chin. "I'm sorry I misjudged you, Sally. Let's be friends." She held out her hand and the little dog sealed the bargain by licking the icing off Brooke's fingers.

It was two hours later when the party finally ended. As they waved goodbye to their last guests, the twins felt tired and happy. "You know what?" Jessica told her sister. "That was the nicest party I've ever been to, even if we did give it ourselves!"

"It sure was," agreed Elizabeth. "And the

best part is we can spend the whole school day tomorrow just being us."

Suddenly Jessica's face darkened. "And the worst part is," she reminded her twin, "we haven't done our homework."

"Oh, no!" Both girls looked helplessly at the paper and food strewn across the living room. "We'll never get this mess cleaned up in time to study for that big history test!"

"Yes, you will," Mr. Wakefield assured them. "Your mother and I will form a clean-up brigade while you two get down to work." He turned to Steven, who had already started upstairs with his sisters. "As for you, Steven, there's a certain little dog that needs to be returned to Mrs. Bramble."

"Oh, Dad." Steven headed reluctantly for the hall, Sally bouncing eagerly behind him. "It doesn't pay to be the scholarly type like me and finish your homework early!" He grabbed a taco, gathered up Sally's leash, and was out the door.

Elizabeth had been at work only a few minutes when the usual knock at the door interrupted her. "Hi, Liz." Jessica flung herself onto Elizabeth's bed, anxious to talk about the party. For once, Elizabeth didn't mind. She felt too grateful and excited to concentrate on Greek mythology.

"Jess, I think things are really going to be different for Brooke from now on."

Jessica grinned at her twin. "Yep," she agreed. "And the difference won't be just in the way she dresses either."

"Mom said she and Mr. Dennis had a long talk." Elizabeth left her desk to sit beside her sister on the bed. "He says he's going to take some time off for a while. He's going to spend more time with Brooke and do some of the work on the house himself."

"That's great, isn't it?" Jessica removed the red bow from her hair and smiled at her twin. "Aren't you proud of us?"

"Proud? Why? We started all the trouble!"

"But if we hadn't, Brooke might still have an absentee father and no friends." Jessica looked suddenly thoughtful. "I wonder if we could help Mary, too."

"Mary?" Elizabeth was puzzled. "Mary Giaccio has tons of friends and a terrific home. What help does she need?"

Jessica pulled her knees up to her chest in her thinking pose. "I wouldn't be too sure of that, Liz. Did you see the way she offered to stay afterwards and help Mom clean up?"

"What's wrong with that?"

"It's unnatural, that's what." At first Elizabeth thought her twin was joking, but the thoughtful frown on Jessica's face made it clear she was in earnest. "I wanted to get her ideas for the Unicorn fund raiser, but all she kept talking about was how great Mom was. You know, how pretty, kind, and—honest. It was really weird."

"Well," Elizabeth told her. "In case you hadn't noticed, we *do* have a pretty neat Mom."

"Sure, but so does Mary."

Elizabeth thought about the Altmans, the friendly couple who were Mary's foster parents. They had a beautiful house and seemed as loving toward Mary as if she were their own child. "Yeah," she admitted, "I like Mrs. Altman a lot."

"That's just what I mean," insisted Jessica. "And why doesn't Mary ever talk about her real parents? I'll bet there's a family mystery behind all this."

"Jessica Wakefield, you've been reading too many Nancy Drew books! Mary is a perfectly ordinary girl with a perfectly nice family."

"Liz, if you'd stop dreaming over those silly horse stories of yours, you'd notice this sort of thing more often!"

Elizabeth laughed. "I know one thing about people *and* animals, Jess. Sometimes it's better to leave them alone than to worry them to death!"

What secret is Mary Giaccio hiding? Find out in Sweet Valley Twins #7, coming next month.

IT ALL STARTED WITH
THE
SWEET VALLEY TWINS

For two years teenagers across the U.S. have been reading about Jessica and Elizabeth Wakefield and their High School friends in SWEET VALLEY HIGH books. Now in books created especially for you, author Francine Pascal introduces you to Jessica and Elizabeth when they were 12, facing the same problems with their folks and friends that you do.

☐ BEST FRIENDS #1   15421/$2.50
☐ TEACHER'S PET #2   15422/$2.50
☐ THE HAUNTED HOUSE #3   15446/$2.50
☐ CHOOSING SIDES #4   15459/$2.50
☐ SNEAKING OUT #5   15474/$2.50
☐ THE NEW GIRL #6   15475/$2.50
☐ THREE'S A CROWD #7   15500/$2.50
☐ FIRST PLACE #8   15510/$2.50
☐ AGAINST THE RULES #9   15518/$2.50

Bantam Books, Inc., Dept. SVT, 414 East Golf Road, Des Plaines, Ill. 60016

Please send me the books I have checked above. I am enclosing $_____ (please add $1.50 to cover postage and handling). Send check or money order—no cash or C.O.D.s please.

Mr/Ms _____

Address _____

City/State _____ Zip _____

SVT—6/87

Please allow four to six weeks for delivery. This offer expires 12/87.